LOST AND FOUND

THE KELLER FAMILY SERIES ~ BOOK FIVE

BERNADETTE MARIE

5 PRINCE PUBLISHING

Lost and Found

ISBN Digital: 978-1-939217-54-7

ISBN Print: 978-1-63112-311-5

4th edition

5 Prince Publishing, LLC

PO Box 865, Arvada CO 80001

books@5princebooks.com

Published by 5 Prince Publishing

To Stan,
Whenever I was lost,
you were always there to find me.

ACKNOWLEDGMENTS

To my husband and our fantastic 5:

Your amazing support and love help me write every one of these stories. I am blessed to know what family is all about.

To Mom, Dad, and NitNat:

What would the Keller Family be if I didn't understand family dynamics? Thank you for giving me a wonderful family.

To Connie:

The "family" that brought us together taught us a lot. And funny how we became so close outside that "family circle." You're my right hand, my left arm, my brain at times. I thank you.

To Kelyn, Connie, Sandy, Jill, Missy, Amy, and Holly:

So many of you have been "my family" in one way or another. Some I grew up with, some I met through martial arts, others through my husband. Family is so strong. Thank you for helping me make this family saga so incredible.

ALSO BY BERNADETTE MARIE

Date for Hire

LOST AND FOUND

CHAPTER 1

*E*d Keller leaned back in his chair and kicked his feet up on his desk. The view from his office would never cease to amaze him. The view from his uncle's office was much more spectacular, but he had no reason to complain.

Who would have thought, nearly twenty years ago when he'd asked for an after-school job to afford a limo ride to take a girl to prom, that he'd end up with the title Vice President on his business cards.

He laughed. He couldn't even think of the girl's name that had squeezed at his heart. She'd been older. That he remembered. But he'd never done well with older women.

Now he sat atop an empire that his uncle's grandfather had started and his uncle's father had carried on. But it was Zach Benson, his uncle, who made it what it was today.

Benson, Benson, and Hart built big—built on time—and built under budget. Nothing had changed.

Ed didn't have a foreman like Zach had. His other uncle, John Forrester, had been the best foreman any company could have asked for. A loyal employee until Ed's Aunt Arianna made him retire only two years earlier. But another would come along. Right now he had to focus on a new assistant.

Interviewing people for a position shouldn't be an issue. He'd been doing it for years. But a personal assistant had to be in your business, and he didn't like that.

He'd fought it for years. Temps were good. They came, did the work, and left. He figured it was kind of like dating the wrong girl. There weren't any he wanted to spend his life with.

Perhaps his expectations were too high. After all, his Aunt Regan had been Zach's assistant. They'd been married nearly twenty-five years, and she still took care of him. It wouldn't be long before Tyler and Spencer, their sons, would be sitting in Ed's seat.

Ed dropped his feet to the floor and pushed up from his chair. When the time was right, he'd find the assistant of his dreams. He'd given up on the woman of his dreams, so an assistant would have to do.

He walked to the elevator and pressed the button to go down to the lobby. There was a Starbucks there now, and he'd grown very fond of caramel lattes, thanks to his Aunt Arianna, though he didn't go for the skinny version. His Uncle John would say it was a bit too frilly a drink for a man in the construction business. His Uncle Zach, on the other hand, would argue that it was a good stress reliever.

Ed laughed at himself. What an eclectic bunch of people he had in his family. And even without them there with him, he still enjoyed them.

The gathering of the masses in the Starbucks also entertained him, almost as much as the thoughts of his family and their differences.

Ed ordered his drink and stood at the counter waiting for it to be handed to him.

As he looked around the store, he mentally spotted and named each kind of person. There was the tourist, the executive, and the assistant. There was a couple, obviously just downtown for the day and…hmmm, one that stumped him.

She was professional, probably interviewing by the way she was dressed, but she wasn't comfortable with the big building and the mass of people. She was using Starbucks as a common ground, something familiar, to ease her nerves.

He listened as she ordered her drink—decaf and nonfat. What fun was in that, he wondered.

She tucked her change back into her purse, walked to the end of the counter, and stood behind Ed to wait for her drink.

Flowery perfume filled his nose. She had a sweet side.

The lady behind the counter handed Ed his iced caramel latte. He turned to leave and, he'd say so himself, that was when things got interesting.

The woman who had been standing behind him, searching in her bag for something, looked up just as Ed turned around. She shifted to move out of his way, but instead she moved right into him.

Ed's hands slipped from the condensation on the cup, and the entire, cold drink poured down the front of the woman.

She let out a stifled scream, and her hands went into the air. "Oh-my-God!"

"I'm very sorry."

Ed turned toward the counter and grabbed a handful of napkins. He would have helped to mop up her clothes, but he noticed that the white, silk shirt clung to her and decided it just wasn't a good idea to try.

"Look what you did!" She ripped the napkins from his hand and began to blot away the coffee, which had already stained the shirt.

"Sorry, but I think you ran into me."

She snapped her head up again. "Oh, men. You're not always right, you know. Sometimes you do make mistakes."

Not only was she not as sweet as her flowery perfume, she was jaded. Bad news.

"Again, I'm very sorry. How can I help you?" He turned and reached for more napkins, but when she pulled them from his hand, he noticed she was crying.

"I think you've done enough."

"I still think I can help in some way."

"Listen. My suit is ruined. This is the only one I have. I was searching for a job, and I can't do that now. I can't hand out resumes looking like this."

Ed watched as the woman continued to wipe off her blouse, but to no avail. It was ruined, but he still wasn't going to take the blame.

"Are you looking for a job in this building?"

She let out a grunt. "Why else would I be here?"

"I was just asking. I know most of the businesses in the building. Perhaps I can help you out."

The woman pursed her lips. "I don't need your charity."

"It's not charity. You seem to be in need of a job, and I'm sure I can help you find one."

"What, do you own this place?" She waved her arms in the air.

"Let me see your resume."

The woman stared at him as if he'd lost his mind. That wasn't new. You didn't run a multi-million dollar company in your mid-thirties without people giving you a shifty eye.

Her coffee was set on the counter. He moved in to grab it, but she moved quicker. "I'll get this. I can't afford to waste a sip of this. It's my breakfast and lunch."

She picked up the coffee and moved to a table where she set down the cup and pulled a resume from her bag. She handed it to Ed. "Here it is. I hate to say it, but I'm desperate. If I don't find a job in three days, I have to go home."

"Why? Does that suit turn back into a pumpkin and your glass slipper breaks?"

"Have you ever been desperate for anything in your life?"

He didn't have anything to say. The only desperate thing he'd ever done was ask his uncle for a job at fifteen so he could get that limo to go to prom. Look where it landed him twenty years later. She was right. He'd never been desperate for anything.

"How do you feel about assistant work for a commercial builder?"

"You actually know of a job?"

"I actually know of a job." He folded her resume and tucked it into his pocket. "Ed Keller is an executive at Benson, Benson, and Hart. He needs an assistant."

Her face went pale, and her lips parted. This reaction went beyond her reaction to his spilling his drink on her. "That was the business I was going to leave my resume with."

"You're into architecture?"

He watched as she swallowed hard, but the color hadn't returned to her cheeks yet. "Not exactly, but do you think you can get me in there?"

"I'm sure I can."

She nodded and picked up her coffee. "You don't think Mr. Keller will mind my attire?"

Ed smiled. "I guarantee he will be fine. Your resume is impressive. I'm sure that he'd understand that accidents happen."

She nodded again, nervously. "I'm still mad that you ruined my suit."

"And I'm sorry that you bumped into me. But if you'll come with me, I'll get you a job. And, if you're hungry for lunch later, there is a hot dog cart out back. I'd love to buy you some lunch."

CHAPTER 2

$\mathcal{D}$arcy watched the elevator doors close. She was alone with the man who had ruined her day, but also had offered her an opportunity. She was scared to death.

She'd planned this day for so long. Now she was in the building, and she was headed to the company offices of Benson, Benson, and Hart.

Her heart pounded in her chest. She hadn't expected this. It was in her plans, but as the doors opened to the floor, and the name was before her on the wall in big, shiny letters, she thought she might just throw up.

She only knew one thing about herself—her past—and it had led her to Benson, Benson, and Hart. She'd planned to attempt to, at least, get in the door since all the other jobs she'd applied for had fallen through. The journey to find out about herself wasn't supposed to drop her in the office where she knew her all her answers would lie. This was supposed to be months down the road when she'd had time to explore more about herself and where she'd come from. Now what?

The man exited the elevator and looked at her. "Are you coming?"

"I seem to be very nervous." Which kept her planted on the elevator.

He reached for her hand and pulled her gently from the elevator. He took off his suit coat and draped it over her shoulders. It was a courteous move to hide the huge stain on her blouse, which she knew she'd caused because she wasn't paying attention, but she still wasn't going to let him think he didn't do it. Men would use you if you weren't careful.

The man led her to an office, and the name on the door read EDUARDO KELLER. She sucked in a breath as he opened the door and walked in.

"Have a seat." He pointed to the chairs in front of the desk.

Darcy took a seat, set her bag to the side, and then slid her arms through the sleeves of the jacket he'd draped on her. She probably looked ridiculous. He was at least six feet tall and broad shouldered. She wasn't very tall at all, and she didn't even come close to filling out the jacket.

The man sat behind the desk and turned on the computer monitor.

"Should you be doing that?" she asked.

"I need to find the application information to fill out for the human resource department."

"You're going to fill it out?"

"I usually do when I'm hiring people."

She looked around the office. Eduardo Keller had no personal affects. The man must be all business.

"Why are you doing the hiring?"

The man stopped what he was doing. He folded his hands on the top of the desk and gazed at her with dark brown eyes.

"Because I'm Ed Keller."

· · ·

Ed had seen his share of angry women in his life. When this woman's face turned the color of Santa's suit, he knew he'd crossed the line.

She stood from the chair and grabbed her bag. "Do you think this is funny? You're messing with my life."

"Whoa." He stood from his seat. "Calm down."

"Calm down? I will not calm down."

"I've seen your resume. You're very qualified for the position I need to fill, and I'd like to help you."

"Help me?" She lifted the bag onto her shoulder. "Help me? Why would you want to do that? You're just some stuck-up executive who can play with people, like spilling coffee on a woman to get her into your office. Is this what you do here?"

Ed planted his hands firmly on his desk and looked at her. "You told me you had three days to find a job. You told me I ruined all your chances by messing up your blouse. So you can either hear me out, or you can leave here with your stained clothing, your wrinkled resume, and your bad attitude and find a job."

The woman sucked in a breath and let it out slowly. "What is the job?"

"Executive assistant."

"To you?"

"Yes."

Her shoulders dropped, and she bit her bottom lip. She was contemplating, but he didn't know, in his own heart, which way he wanted her to go now. It was very likely he'd just made a big mistake offering it to her if she was so volatile.

The woman set her bag back on the ground and extended her hand to him. "Darcy McCary, your new assistant."

Darcy studied Eduardo Keller as he shook her hand. Was he happy? Mad? Oh, he'd been messing with her, and now she really felt stupid. But she needed the job, and he was right—she was very qualified. She needed to find an apartment and establish some savings. Private investigators hadn't been cheap, and she couldn't tell her father that she'd hired them. God, if only the person she'd set out to find had done a DNA test, things would be so much easier.

She had a debt to pay and a life to understand—her life.

Darcy McCary was in Tennessee to find her birth mother, and the investigator told her that all ties led to Nashville and to Benson, Benson, and Hart.

CHAPTER 3

*D*arcy had accepted the job, and now walked out the front door of the Riverside Building into the early July heat.

Eduardo Keller had told her to come back in the morning, and he would personally see that human resources got her processed first thing. He said they had a lot of work to do.

Darcy walked around the side of the building to a courtyard that overlooked the river. She noticed the hot dog stand and realized that Eduardo Keller had also promised her lunch. He must have forgotten that part.

She opened her purse and pulled out her wallet. That Starbucks coffee had cost her nearly her last dime, but it had landed her a job. But she was starving. Maybe she could find the three dollars for a hot dog.

She was in luck. Stuck behind an Old Navy credit card, which wasn't even active since she'd forgotten to pay the bill on time, there was a five dollar bill. She pulled it out and headed to the stand that said Frank and Sons.

"What can I get ya?"

She looked over the menu. "I think just a regular dog, please."

"Anything else?"

She looked at the five dollar bill wadded in her hand. "No, that'll do."

As the vendor went about getting her hot dog, she felt someone walk up behind her. She didn't turn to look, but the man behind the cart gave a nod.

"The usual, Ed?"

"You bet. And I'm paying for hers, too."

Darcy turned and noticed Eduardo Keller standing right behind her. "You don't need to do that."

"I think the deal was I'd get you a job and buy you a hot dog."

"So, you did remember that?" She turned back to toward the cart and took the hot dog as the man handed it to her.

"Frank, get us each a soda and a bag of chips, too." He walked up next to her and pulled two napkins out of the dispenser. "You can't have a dog without soda and chips."

"You can if you're being conservative."

He only nodded as he reached for his hot dog. Frank handed them each a soda, and they pulled their chips from the display.

"There's a table over there." He pointed toward the river with his elbow.

Darcy followed him to the table, and they both sat down.

She'd always loved Nashville, though she'd only been a few times. Her parents never seemed to want to be there too long, and she guessed it had something to do with the fact that perhaps her birth mother was there. It was a mystery to her. Maybe they didn't even know her birth mother.

She looked up to see Eduardo watching her.

He opened his soda. "You look like you have a lot going on in that head of yours."

"I usually do. My father says I have more conversations with myself than I do with other people."

He found that amusing as he bit into his hot dog. "That keeps you company then, right?"

"I guess."

She took her first bite into the hot dog. She hadn't realized just how hungry she was until she'd sat down to eat.

"Thank you for lunch," she said, covering her full mouth.

"You're welcome. Thank you for ending my search for an assistant. I was seriously dreading having to give it more thought."

She wasn't sure that was very positive. "Have the applicants been bad?"

He shook his head. "No. I just have a hard time with finding one I want to keep around. Maybe I have a personality flaw."

A crude comment came right to mind, but she pushed it back. "I'll do my best. I promise."

"I know you will. You can tell when someone needs a job and will do the job. Trust me, after this many years, I've seen every kind of employee out there."

"How long have you been at this company?"

"Twenty years. My first job was working a site after school when I was fifteen. My uncle, well he wasn't my uncle then, but he used to have me work with a different kind of craftsman every week. I thought he was just trying to keep me busy. But, in reality, he was teaching me every job on a site."

"He sounds like a very smart man."

"Oh, he is. The first job he gave me was to design an office for my aunt. It was a masterpiece. She loved it."

"How old were you?"

"I was just about sixteen. I wish we had some pictures of it."

Darcy opened her soda and took a sip. "She doesn't work in it anymore?"

"It burnt down just days after I got it done."

She watched him as he talked about it. He didn't seem too

saddened by the loss, but she could see it had been a big deal to him at the time.

"Did you design her a new one?"

"You bet I did. It was even better." That brought the glimmer back to his dark eyes.

"What about you? You said if you didn't find a job you'd have to go home. Where is that?"

"Kentucky."

"Oh, you're not too far from home then."

"Far enough." The pang of guilt and sadness was just enough to bring tears to her eyes that she batted away quickly.

"So, why come to Nashville for a job?"

"Something I had to do." She wasn't going to tell him that somewhere within the organization of Benson, Benson, and Hart the truth to who she was lay hidden—and for the time being, it was hidden from her, too.

The private investigator got her that far, but without more funds, he wouldn't keep searching. At this point, she was on her own.

"You also said you needed a place to live." He opened his bag of Doritos and crunched one between his teeth.

"Yes. I'm on my last two days at the motel."

"I know of a nice basement apartment just about twenty minutes from here."

"Really?" This guy really was into helping people, or he had an ulterior motive.

"My aunt has a house with a very nice basement apartment. My brother lives upstairs right now—when he's in town."

"He travels a lot?"

"He's a semi-professional baseball player."

"No kidding?" This guy had an amazing group of people he knew. Already he'd mentioned aunts, uncles, brothers...who else did he know?

"Do you have a car?"

16

Darcy shook her head. She'd sold it to pay for her trip.

"Well, it's on a bus line, and I know for a fact the bus comes straight here. The rent is decent if you'd like to look at it."

She'd be a fool not to accept the offer to look at it. After all, at eleven the next morning she was going to be homeless.

"I'd like that."

"Let's finish lunch, and we'll head over and take a look."

CHAPTER 4

$\mathcal{D}$arcy sat quietly in his black GMC Yukon Denali. She was taking in all the little things about Eduardo Keller that she could gather without asking.

He'd been working hard since he was fifteen, so his executive status was deserved.

He'd mentioned uncles and aunts and a brother, so he came from a larger family, she assumed.

The truck still said Tennessee, even if it said classy, too. Darcy's father had an old, green Ford from the early eighties which was his pride and joy, but dang, it was old. She rather enjoyed a man who had a classy, yet manly side.

Darcy turned her head and looked out the window. There was no need to enjoy anything about this man. It was just coincidence that the very man that ruined her suit happened to work at the company she needed to get into.

A pang of guilt pierced her chest, and she moved her shoulders to try and ease it. She was going to have to use this man to help her, but he really couldn't know. Somewhere within the organization, someone knew something about her birth mother.

If she played her cards right, Eduardo could lead her right to that person.

Darcy wasn't a game player, but she could be if there was a chance she'd win the game. And this game was solving a mystery —her mystery.

She turned to look at him. "It's very pretty out here."

"I know. I've traveled all over the world, but Tennessee has its own beauty, and I don't think I could live anywhere else."

"So you've lived here your whole life."

"Yep. What about you?"

"I've lived in Kentucky my whole life. I was born in Nashville though."

"Really? So your folks lived here for a little bit?" He turned the truck down a residential street.

"No." There was no need to go into intimate details.

Eduardo pulled up in front of a small, well-kept house. Out front, an American flag blew in the slight breeze. She liked that— a house with a flag said home to her.

Eduardo climbed out of the truck and hurried to her side. He opened the door before she even realized he'd gone around the truck.

"Thank you."

He held his hand up to her to help her out. "My pleasure."

The front door of the house opened, and a man resembling Eduardo stepped out onto the porch. He had a lighter complexion and a goatee, but this was obviously his brother.

"What, are you slacking?" the man asked as he walked down the stairs.

"I'm working. Possible tenant."

Darcy climbed out of the truck as the man walked toward them.

"Darcy, this is my brother, Christian," Eduardo introduced them.

"Nice to meet you," Christian said as he shook her hand.

"Likewise."

He watched her carefully as if he knew her secret already, but she knew that was impossible.

"Do I know you?" he finally asked.

"I'm certain you don't. I'm from Kentucky."

Christian nodded. "You just look very familiar." He studied her for a moment longer and then turned back to his brother. "I was just headed out. Clara needs something lifted into place at the theater, and Tyler and I have been volunteered."

Eduardo laughed. "Clara is our sister, and Tyler is our cousin."

She nodded, taking it all in. "You have an enormous family, don't you?"

"Enormous and eclectic." He laughed, and Christian followed suit.

"I'll leave you two to the house," Christian said as he headed to the driveway. "Nice to meet you, Darcy."

Eduardo led her to the side of the house where there was a paved path that led to an outside stairwell.

"My aunt owned the house before she moved to New York and worked on Broadway. My uncle ended up renting the basement, and he fixed it up beautifully. That was twenty years ago, but since Benson, Benson, and Hart maintain the property, it has stayed nice. Besides, it's usually been family that lived here over the years."

They walked down the stairs, and Eduardo unlocked the door.

"Your aunt was on Broadway?"

He pushed the door open. "She sure was. Now she has a theater downtown. My sister works hand-in-hand with her on the productions. Clara is one amazingly talented woman. I think she should become a recording artist, but she's happy where she is."

It was a lot to take in for Darcy. After all, she was an only child to older parents. It wasn't until two years before her mother died that she'd even found out that she was adopted. She felt as though she'd missed out on so much.

There was a pang of jealousy that twitched in her belly. Did Eduardo Keller know how lucky he was?

He turned on the lights to the small basement apartment, and she knew that moment that this was her new home.

"Wow, this is not what I expected when you said basement apartment."

He chuckled. "What did you have in mind?"

"Oh, you know, the basement of some freaky old guy's house like in college. But the rent was usually right."

"The price is right here, too."

"Can I afford it on my new paycheck?"

"I can even have it drafted out for you weekly."

That was a bonus, she thought. "Here's the problem. I can't do a first and last month rent. Can you work with me?"

Eduardo crossed his arms in front of him. "How about this? In lieu of the first month rent, you give me some forgiveness for ruining your blouse."

"Really?"

"I could change my mind," he said as he walked toward the kitchen.

"I forgive you."

"Good. Now let me show you the rest of the place."

CHAPTER 5

*D*arcy folded her clothes, which she had just pulled from the dryer at the motel, and laid them neatly into her suitcase. She reached for the remote to the TV, turned down the volume, and then picked up her phone and called her father.

"Daddy, I got a job and found a cute place to live."

He let out a low growl. "A cute place to live?"

Darcy chuckled. "The company I went to work for is a commercial builder, and they have this house they manage. I'm renting the basement."

"Darcy, I don't like…"

"I know." She cut him off and sat down on the bed. "I'm fine, Daddy. I want to make this work."

She heard his disapproving growl again.

"Why did you have to leave Kentucky? There are lots of jobs here, too."

She wondered if he was really on to her. He was quick like that, but he hadn't said a word—yet.

"I just feel like this is where I need to be. Listen, I'll call you tomorrow with the address."

"Do you need some money?"

She smiled. He was always practical, that was for sure.

"Well, since you asked."

EDUARDO HAD GIVEN HER THE KEY TO THE APARTMENT AND TOLD her that anytime she wanted to bring her stuff over she could. He'd have his uncle do a run through on everything and make sure the apartment was in perfect working order. He assured her they'd sign the lease in the morning.

She had to admit, the moment she laid eyes on Eduardo Keller, despite his very sexy charm, his dark eyes, and that low mesmerizing voice, she'd hated him.

He'd nearly ruined everything she was trying to do.

But as she looked around the basement apartment, she realized fate had a funny way of presenting itself. If only finding her birth mother would be as easy.

Darcy was on her own there. She couldn't afford anymore investigators. She'd have to use what information she had. At least she knew she'd landed in the right spot. If she got in good enough with Eduardo Keller, she'd soon enough meet whomever she was supposed to meet who would lead her to her mother.

Then it occurred to her that maybe the path didn't lead to her mother, but maybe to her father.

She felt her shoulders tense. That hadn't crossed her mind, and she wondered why it hadn't. It had all been about a birth mother. She hadn't really given too much thought on her birth father—but there had to be one. And obviously he hadn't done a public DNA test either that matched them.

Darcy turned as she heard steps on the stairs, and she realized she'd left the door open so she could bring in her few bags.

An older gentleman stood at the door looking in.

"You Darcy?"

"I am."

"John Forrester. Ed's uncle."

She had to process for a moment and then realized that Eduardo would be called Ed by his family.

"Nice to meet you. Come in."

"Place still looks the same," he said as he untied his boots and slipped them off by the door, then laid his jacket atop them. "Ed wants me to just check and make sure it's all in order for you."

"Thank you."

John started with the windows and making sure the seals were good. He double checked the door in the kitchen that would go up to the house, she figured. He ran water in the kitchen and bathroom. Everything that he could possibly look at, he'd done.

"I think you're set," he said.

"So you're the uncle who lived here and fixed up the apartment?"

"I am."

"Eduardo has mentioned his family a lot already. It seems you are all very important to him."

John slipped his feet into his boots and then knelt down to tie them.

"The Keller family is a very tight-knit family. We fill two rooms with tables come Thanksgiving." He chuckled and stood back up. "My wife and I are the only two without children, but her sister and brothers made up for that." He slipped on his jacket.

"Do you all live in Tennessee?"

"For now. I'm sure Christian," he pointed up, "will have to leave to play major league someday. Clara, she's almost too talented to stay here, but then again," he shrugged, "she's a singer and this is Nashville. Avery has citizenship in France, too. You never know where she'll land. And someday, I assume Tyler and Spencer will take over the empire."

"What empire?"

"Benson, Benson, and Hart."

"Oh!" Things were quickly falling into place. She hadn't realized that Eduardo was family—nepotism was an interesting thing. When he'd said his uncle had started him working on the sites, she didn't think that uncle had anything to do with Benson, Benson, and Hart from the inside.

A ruined blouse and a spilled coffee might have landed her in just the right spot. The nephew to the owner was her boss. Surely he could help her find out anything and everything about the people who worked for the company.

John looked around. "Can I help you move anything in?"

Darcy wrinkled up her nose. "I don't have anything."

"I beg your pardon? What are you going to sleep on?"

She shrugged. "The floor, I guess. Things moved a bit faster than I thought." She wrung her hands together. "My father is sending some money to help me get settled. So for a few days I'll be fine."

John grumbled. "Are you sticking around for a few hours?"

She smiled. "I'll be home all night."

"I'll be back," he said as he turned and walked away.

Darcy shut the door. What did that mean?

CHAPTER 6

Two hours later, Darcy found out what John Forrester had meant when she opened the door and found him and Ed standing just beyond it with a mattress.

"What's this?" she asked as she stepped back.

John shook his head. "You can't sleep on the floor. That has never flown with me."

He moved past her carrying one end of the mattress and Eduardo had the other. They walked through the living room and straight to the bedroom.

"Hi," another voice said from the door as the men passed through. "I'm Arianna, John's wife and Ed's aunt."

"Darcy."

"Nice to meet you." Arianna looked at her with that same familiar glint in her eye as Christian had, but then continued, "I hope you don't mind us barging in. John is a bit of a caretaker. He said you didn't have anything, so he rounded up some items to get you settled. These are for you." She handed her a bag of groceries and a set of sheets.

"I can't believe you'd all do this for me."

"The Keller family stands by each other. Ed hired you and must think enough to do so. So consider yourself one of us."

That stuck in her chest. Someone considered her part of their family after only a few hours?

She didn't want to cry, but it was coming.

Arianna moved to her and touched her shoulder. "Are you okay?"

"I lost my mom this past year. I don't have any brothers or sisters or even cousins, so your generosity is a bit overwhelming."

"You sent her into tears?" Eduardo asked as he came around the corner. "Listen, I did that this morning. We're not winning her over very well, and I already hired her."

Darcy laughed. "I'm fine. This is amazing. In one day, I hated you and then got a job, lunch, a house, and now all this."

"Oh, yeah, that's how we work."

"I see that."

John took the sheets from her. "I'll put these on. Sorry we don't have a frame, but by tomorrow…" he said as he disappeared into the bedroom.

Arianna took the bag of groceries from her. "I'll put these in the kitchen."

"I can't believe you all did this."

Eduardo's forehead wrinkled when he lifted his brows. "You said that."

She sighed. "Thank you."

Eduardo tucked his thumbs into the front pockets of his jeans and rocked back on his heels. "Before they fill this place, do you have furniture coming?"

The smile that had permeated her lips disappeared. "No. My dad is sending some money, but…"

"Okay, good. As soon as I told one person in my family that I had a renter, suddenly all sorts of items became available. Assuming you don't mind him having the key, by the time you get home from work tomorrow, your house will be furnished."

The tears were back, and Eduardo took a step back.

"Sorry. I was telling your aunt I don't have a big family. It's only my dad and I now, so this is very overwhelming."

"I see." Eduardo rubbed the back of his neck. "Since you're new to town I'd assume you don't have any plans tonight?"

"None."

"There's the barbecue place I've had a hankering for. Interested in getting a bite to eat?"

"Are you sure you want to take your assistant out for another meal? I don't want you to think I'm needy."

He laughed. "Let's just say I still feel guilty for spilling on you."

"It wasn't your fault."

"I know," he said and Darcy let out a groan.

FOR THE SECOND TIME IN A DAY, DARCY WAS SEATED IN THE BIG truck, next to a man she just met, who was going to be her boss, but she had yet to do any work. The South was supposed to be slow. Things were known for moving at their own pace, but not with this family.

She felt perfectly at ease with Eduardo—and his aunt and uncle.

"So have you ever lived anywhere else but Kentucky?" Eduardo asked as he merged onto the highway.

"My father was a military doctor when I was born. So we lived in a few places, but I wasn't old enough to remember."

"Like where?"

She gave it some thought. "Germany and Japan."

"That's cool."

Darcy turned in her seat slightly to get a look at the man who had changed her life. There was an exotic look to him. He was dark, his eyes were mysterious, and if she thought about how his T-shirt stretched around his biceps once more, she'd pass out. This was her boss. Not a man to want or to lust over. He was her in at Benson, Benson, and Hart. She needed him so she could find what she came for and then get out.

"What about you? Ever lived anywhere else?"

Eduardo shook his head. "I lived with my parents. Then when they got divorced, I lived between them. One week here. One week there. Then when they got remarried, I lived with them again. Did my time in a college dorm. Then I lived in the house you live in now, but upstairs for a few years. And now I live in the house my grandparents lived in for fifty years."

"Is that your way of saying you never left Tennessee?"

"Yup."

She settled back against her seat and laughed. "So your parents divorced and remarried? Each other?"

This time he chuckled. "Yes. I was ten when they split. They just weren't getting along anymore. Mom married Dad's best friend. Then Dad got engaged when Matt, my stepfather, left my mom and she found out she had cancer."

"Oh. My mother died of cancer," her voice dipped.

His head snapped to her, and his eyes had gone sad. "I'm so sorry." She knew it was instinct and a trait of a caring man when he reached across the cab and gave her hand a squeeze. "When did she pass?"

"Last year."

"I can't imagine losing my mother. Though in my head, I did it a million times that year to prepare myself."

"How is she now?"

He smiled. "Healthier than ever."

"So, how did they get back together?"

"Oh, yeah." He checked his mirrors and exited the highway. "Well, it was an interesting few years. They got divorced and Mom remarried, but she and my dad were always great friends. When she got sick, he was right by her side. It blossomed after that. But it was his new wife, of one day mind you, who sent him to get my mom back. Even she knew they should be together."

"Your dad was married for one day?"

He nodded. "Kathy. She was a nice lady, but not perfect for dad. She knew it. But now she's married and has three kids. That was what she wanted. I'm happy for her."

"You said you live in your grandparents' house. Did they pass?"

"No. They moved into a retirement home about ten years ago. They are in their nineties, so having someone around all the time is good for them. But you wouldn't know they were that old. They play cards every day. Go for walks. My grandpa, now that we're all older, tells the dirtiest jokes, but I don't think grandma knows he tells us."

"Wanna bet?" She laughed, and he turned to look at her. "Old women let old men have their way, but they still have the power."

"Experience?"

"Older parents."

"I see."

CHAPTER 7

*E*duardo pulled into the parking lot of Steve's Barbecue Pit and Beer.

"This is where you wanted to take me for dinner?" Darcy laughed when she saw the sign.

"Trust me, you'll be begging for me to take you again."

He turned off the engine and jumped out of the truck. Darcy gathered her purse, and by the time she turned to open the door, Eduardo pulled it open and held out his hand to help her down.

"Why do southern men have big trucks?" she asked.

"So we look like gentlemen when we help ladies out of them."

"Rather than see us fall?"

"It's never pretty," he said as he shut the door, and they walked toward the restaurant.

Darcy was met with an array of smells. Stale beer and barbecue were top note scents and next came fresh bread. She'd been hungry, but now she was starving.

Country music played on a jukebox. It was old country, too. Patsy Cline. Her mother loved Patsy Cline.

The walls were decorated to the hilt with garage sale finds. Some items still had price tags.

The hostess sat them at a booth and set both sets of silverware and the menus on one side of the table.

"I guess she assumes we're together," Darcy said.

"It would be a common thought. A man and a woman out to dinner. We certainly aren't dressed for talking business."

He motioned for her to take a seat, and then he sat on the booth across from her, pulling the menu and silverware wrap toward him.

"Are you up for ribs?" he asked.

"Sure."

"They have a dinner for two, if that's okay."

Darcy set the menu down. "Sounds fine."

"Also comes with a pitcher of beer. But you can have whatever you want."

"Beer sounds fine."

When the waitress came to collect their orders, Eduardo ordered for them and then sat back against the booth and looked around as though he were taking in the atmosphere.

"Do you come here a lot?" she asked.

"Nah. Once in a great while. But my dad brought us when I was about eleven. Uncle John had brought him. It's an old BBH tradition, I guess."

"BBH?"

"Benson, Benson, and Hart."

"Oh." She eased back in the booth. "Did your dad work there, too?"

"Just for a short time. Aunt Regan got him the job when he was between teaching positions."

"Your dad is a teacher?"

"Yep. Well, he was. He's a school district administrator now."

"That sounds official."

The waitress brought their pitcher of beer and two frosty mugs. Eduardo moved in and pulled the mugs toward him. "Do you mind if I pour?"

"That's fine, thanks."

"Some women are very independent, so I don't want to step on any toes."

"Well, as we're not on a date, and I like a tad bit of chivalry anyway, you don't have to impress me, and I appreciate the gesture."

Eduardo poured their beers and slid one toward her. Then he lifted his mug as to make a toast. "To our new working relationship. May you be able to keep up with my demands…"

"And may you not seem too demanding," she finished the toast.

They tapped glasses and each took a sip from their mugs.

Darcy set hers down. "I'm still trying to learn this family of yours. So your uncle owns the company?"

He smiled. "My uncle Zach owns the company. His grandfather started it, and it was passed to his father and then to him."

"But now you run it?"

"No. I run some of the builds. It'll go to his sons someday. I consider it that I'm just helping to sustain it until then."

"And Uncle Zach is married to?"

"Aunt Regan. She was his assistant. In fact, they met the morning she was supposed to start her new job. She was soaking wet from a flash rain storm and had to take the bus because my dad was fixing her car. Well, he had run home that night, literally. He's a big runner.

"So he was on the bus, too. But when the bus jolted, she fell right into his lap."

"That's how they met?"

"Yep. Then he brought her here for dinner on one of her first nights that they were working."

She felt an uneasy similarity happening between them, and she wasn't sure she liked that. She quickly lifted her beer to her mouth and took a big chug.

"How long have they been married?"

Eduardo calculated in his head. "Twenty-three years, I think."

"Guess it worked out for them," she said, then took another sip of her beer.

"Well, the marriage did. He fired her."

Darcy choked on her drink and set the mug down as she coughed. "He fired her?"

"She lost him a big contract."

"Oh." Panic took over her body, and as she reached for her beer, she noticed her hand was shaking. She pulled it back. "How did she do that?"

"She didn't really. It was a bad business deal, and she got caught in the middle. But, as a family joke, we say that's how it went down."

Darcy wasn't sure she understood. "All of these aunts and uncles are from your dad's family?"

"Yep. My mom's not as close to her family. But the Kellers— they're a tight bunch."

"Sounds that way."

The waitress came back with their plates of ribs and bread.

Darcy's eyes widened when she saw the amount of food before them.

"Is this normal? Did you invite anyone else?"

He laughed. "No, this is it. We'll box up the leftovers, and you can take them home for tomorrow."

Darcy smiled as Eduardo handed her a roll. She liked him. It was a far better feeling than the one she'd had that morning. But then again, her luck seemed to be changing the longer she was around him. Maybe it would be good to be his assistant and get to know the rest of the Kellers. They might not be her family, but until she found what she was looking for, she sure could use a dose of friendship from one.

CHAPTER 8

*A*s Darcy finished getting ready for the day, she heard a knock on the door.

For not having any friends in Tennessee, she sure received a lot of visitors.

Christian stood there in a pair of running shorts and a sleeveless T-shirt. His hair was wet and so was the front of his shirt. His iPhone was latched to his arm with a Velcro band and ear buds dangled around his neck.

"You've already been running?" Darcy asked as she looked him over.

"That was the first run of the day."

"First?"

"Gotta keep in shape."

She laughed. "Would you like to come in? I was just getting ready for work."

"No, no. I just wanted to see if it was okay if I opened the door between here and the house so John could bring over some furniture for you."

"He really doesn't have..."

"You can't tell him that. He'll do it anyway. He's like that."

She smiled. "That would be fine. I'll unlock my side."

He nodded and turned to run back up the stairs. "What time do you have to be to work?"

"Eight. I have to catch the bus by seven."

"Let me get a quick shower, and I'll drive you into town. Then you don't have to leave so early."

He gave her a smile and a nod and ran back up the steps.

Darcy shut the door and went to the kitchen to unlock the door that led to the stairs inside the house.

With Christian driving her to work, she'd save bus fare. She could splurge on a cup of coffee. Yesterday that proved to be an amazing experience. What could happen today, she wondered.

She looked around the kitchen and saw a box of granola bars that Arianna had left for her with the groceries. She opened the box and tasted her first breakfast in her new home.

The day already had started in amazing form. She'd had a good night's rest. She had a job which she was looking forward to. And a handsome man was driving her to work—where an equally handsome man waited. Yes, things were looking up.

CHRISTIAN'S BMW WAS LAVISH, AND HE WAS SKILLED AT maneuvering it between cars with ease as he sped toward town.

"I'm not going to be late," she said as she gripped the door.

"Sorry. Am I making you nervous?"

She just grinned, and he eased the speed of the car.

"I'm usually running late," he said as he shifted lanes again.

"I grew up in a tiny town. One stoplight. All these cars make me nervous anyway."

"I think you'll adjust to city life quick enough. Besides, this city is a lot of fun. It's built on entertainment. Have you checked out any of the bands yet?"

"No. I haven't gotten out much."

He nodded as he exited the highway. "Maybe we can head

downtown one of these nights, and I'll introduce you to the sights and sounds of Nashville. My friend, Randy Seymour, is playing next weekend. Talk about an SOB with talent."

"That would be nice."

Christian pulled into the parking garage at the Riverside Building and collected his parking stub from the machine. He found a space near the elevators and parked.

"I really appreciate you driving me to work, and trust me, I don't expect you to do that every day."

"It was no problem." He opened his door and climbed out of the car and she did the same.

"I'll give you some money for parking."

He waved his hand. "Don't be ridiculous. Ed better validate this, or I'll kick his ass."

She laughed. "You wouldn't really do that, would you?"

"I've been trying for my thirty-three years. I'm in the most fantastic shape. I make a living out of fast objects flying at me, but I'll be damned if I've ever been able to stop a fist to the chest from him. He's just that quick."

"He hits you?"

Christian laughed. "That's the fun of having a brother. Clara flicks your ear. Ya know, that hurts worse." He pushed the button to the elevator and stepped in when the door opened.

She had a lot to learn about family dynamics. That would prove to be as big an adventure as moving to a new city.

Darcy had forgotten about treating herself to a coffee until the doors opened to the floor where Benson, Benson, and Hart had their offices.

She'd do that tomorrow. There was a good chance she'd need it by then. Something told her that she was going to be very overwhelmed.

As Christian turned the corner to Eduardo's office, Darcy had her confirmation.

Eduardo Keller had a very loud voice. At eight in the morning, he could certainly use a very colorful array of words.

Christian's mouth turned up at the corners when he looked back at Darcy, but he didn't stop. He continued to Eduardo's office and pushed open the door.

Darcy followed, but she stopped at the threshold. There was no way she was going into that office.

Eduardo held his cell phone to his ear and paced behind his desk, where stacks of papers were spread all over.

His hair had already been tunneled through with his fingers, numerous times, and his shirt sleeves were pushed up his arms.

Darcy thought she'd shown up to work plenty early. What time did this man get here?

"Are you kidding me? That load was due three days ago. I gave you a little bit of leeway, and you're screwing me over." His voice was steady, but loud. "I have made your company, and you know that. BBH put you in business, and don't think I won't take you out of business. All I have to do is make one call and your mill is gone."

Darcy could see him pace from her safe place in the hallway. Christian, on the other hand, had made himself comfortable on the couch in Eduardo's office. Eduardo didn't seem to mind.

Eduardo nodded and gave a few more grunts. "Valerie, that load had better be on site by two o'clock or I cancel." He nodded again. "Great—now how about dinner?"

Darcy couldn't help but wonder if her jaw literally hit the ground. Had the man been talking to a woman with that mouth? And furthermore, had he just asked her out? Who had she agreed to work for? Well, he'd better never talk to her like that. Her father didn't raise a woman to take crap from anyone—especially some good looking man in a suit who happened to have a great deal of power over her.

The granola bar flipped in her stomach.

Eduardo turned off his phone and looked toward the door.

"Are you going to stay out there all day?"

Darcy stepped in. "I didn't want to interrupt."

"You're going to have to learn. This," he motioned to the phone, "was just another morning."

She wasn't reassured by that.

Eduardo looked at his brother sitting on the couch. "What are you doing here? Come to apply for a real job?"

"You're some kind of funny, huh?" He stood. "I brought your employee to work. I was being neighborly."

She saw him lift his brows playfully, but she was sure she wasn't supposed to see that.

Very quietly, Eduardo spoke, "Don't start."

Christian laughed and pulled the parking stub from his chest pocket. "Validate this before I go."

Eduardo snatched it from his hand. "I'm sure your mother taught you to say please."

"Pleeeease," Christian mimicked, and Eduardo shook his head as he signed the ticket.

Then, at the same time, both men turned to look at her.

Darcy was already nervous enough, but when both sets of dark eyes were staring at her, she didn't know what to think. She was simply mesmerized.

Eduardo was professional, even in his dismantled business suit and mussed up hair. Christian was nearly a spitting image of his brother, only a bit shorter, more defined, laid back, and sporting a goatee. There was something to this duo. A girl could certainly get caught up in those eyes. And to run her fingers through...

What was she doing?

She worked for Eduardo Keller. To even have a momentary lapse of judgment and think thoughts like that was certainly unprofessional. And Christian? She dropped her shoulders. Aside from the fact that they lived in the same house—perhaps he was fair game.

Again, this wasn't why she was here!

CHAPTER 9

$\mathcal{E}$duardo walked back around his desk and shuffled a few papers together. "Chris, will you take her down to personnel?"

"I got her to work and now you want me to get her all hired?"

Eduardo huffed out a breath and sat down in his chair. "I'm busy. Will you help me out?"

Darcy could feel that same anger creeping into her veins as she had when she'd met Eduardo Keller.

"I could find personnel myself," she said, lifting her chin in defiance.

Eduardo only nodded. "He'll take you. And when you're done, get back up here as soon as possible. I'll have Charlie start training you."

Christian started toward her. "Well, if Charlie is going to train..."

Eduardo's head shot up. "Do not come back here, Chris. I'm warning you."

Christian laughed. "Chill out, bro." He took Darcy by the arm and led her down the hall.

"Is he really this temperamental?"

"Ed?" Christian shrugged his shoulders. "Yes."

"Great."

Christian laughed again. "He's about doing business right. He's always been that way. But I think he has a soft spot for you, so don't get too panicked over what you saw."

"Soft spot?"

"Yeah." Christian pushed the button on the elevator. "He's been interviewing for an assistant for a long time. It's a bit too much of a commitment for him to actually hire one. If he has a temp, he can call and fire them through the agency and never have to deal with them. You on the other hand..." The door opened and they stepped into the elevator. When the doors closed, Christian pushed the button. "You got the job after he just met you. He set you up in Arianna's basement. And..." The door opened and he continued, "He didn't kick you out when he started giving Valerie a hard time."

She wasn't sure all of that lead to him having a soft spot for her.

Christian led her to an office that had a much different feel than the offices upstairs. This one reminded her more of a government office, perhaps even the DMV.

"See that man over there?" He pointed to a corner office. "He'll get you squared away."

Darcy nodded.

"Give me your cell phone," Christian said and Darcy handed it to him. He typed something into it, and handed it back to her. "Now you have my contact info. Call me if you need anything."

"Okay. Thank you."

He turned and gave her a small wave. "Oh, and when you see Charlie, say hi for me."

Darcy nodded again and headed toward the office Christian had pointed her to.

· · ·

AN HOUR LATER, DARCY WAS BACK UPSTAIRS. AN OFFICIAL BBH badge was dangled from her neck with her picture on it. And again, she'd forgotten to go down and get a cup of coffee.

Eduardo's office door was closed when she arrived. The desk outside his office was no doubt hers, so she sat down, opened a drawer, and set her purse in it.

Just as she closed the drawer, the door behind her opened, and Eduardo was escorting a very sexy blonde out of his office. His hand was placed on the small of her back, the woman was laughing seductively, and the sight made Darcy nauseous.

This must be Valerie. No wonder he wanted to take her to lunch. She wondered what else they would do on their lunch break.

The very thought infuriated her. This man was disgusting. What was she doing in this job?

However, as the woman walked right past her and down the hall, Eduardo leaned against the doorjamb and scrubbed his hands over his face.

"Do you have any Tylenol?"

Darcy clenched her jaw, opened the drawer with her purse in it, and found him the bottle. She poured out two into her hand and handed them to him.

"Thank you." He put them in his mouth and swallowed dry. "That woman makes my skin crawl."

Darcy looked down the hall where the woman still sauntered past all the offices and then looked back at him.

"Wasn't that Valerie? Aren't you having lunch?"

Eduardo laughed. "That? Valerie?" He leaned against the jamb again and crossed his arms over his chest. "No, that was Charlie."

"Oh," her voice cracked.

"I decided I'd train you. I like you too much to force you to spend time with that woman."

That woman. Wasn't that woman ideal to every man? Hour

glass figure, blonde flowy hair, and ample busts almost popping out of the neckline of her blouse.

It was then that Christian's words flashed back at her. He has a soft spot for you.

She looked up at the man standing in the doorway. He flashed a smile, and her heart rate took off in the upward direction. His dark eyes grew soft as she looked at him. Every bit of her tightened, and she realized, at that very moment, how attracted to him she was.

This was not good.

She was on a mission. She had something to do, and she couldn't get involved with a man who gave her the slightest bit of attention.

But then again, if she felt out this soft spot, maybe she could get the information she was looking for even faster.

ED HAD STARTED DARCY ON PROJECTS THAT HE FIGURED WOULD take her most of the day. It usually took a temp two days, but he was quickly learning that Darcy wasn't like other temps or employees. She'd returned with the purchase orders he'd asked her to fill out within an hour.

"If you see something I've done wrong, please let me know," she said as she handed him the file.

"You're done?"

"Mr. Keller, I take my work seriously."

"Call me Ed."

"Mr.—" She let out a breath. "Eduardo, I..."

"No. Just call me Ed."

Darcy dropped her shoulders. "Ed," she paused on the name. "You had a phone call while you were on a call. Ms. Simone Keller."

"Ah, what did she want?"

"To remind you of the benefit on Saturday night."

Ed slouched in his seat. "Damn, I forgot all about that."

"She sounded French."

That made him smile. "She is. Ever hear of Pierpont Oil?"

"Sure."

"She's the heir."

Darcy nodded slowly and narrowed her brows. "But her last name is Keller. Relative of yours?"

"My aunt."

"Oh, I remember that name. John mentioned her."

He blew out a deep breath. "Do you have a nice dress?"

Darcy's expression changed, and her cheeks turned red. He'd seen that face. Somehow he'd triggered her anger again.

"Why do I need a nice dress? Am I not dressed appropriately?"

"Simmer down. I thought I'd take you with me on Saturday."

"Are you asking me to go to this benefit with you as a guest? Or are you ordering me as an employee?"

Well, she did have a point. Perhaps this was why he didn't have a woman in his life. He sucked at subtly getting his point across.

"I'd like to ask you to accompany me to the benefit on Saturday."

"Then ask me."

Wow, she was a piece of work. "Darcy, would you please be my guest at my aunt's fundraising gala on Saturday?"

"My calendar is empty. I would love to be your guest."

CHAPTER 10

*D*arcy was more than a little surprised to find furniture in her apartment when she returned home. Oh, she'd expected a ratty couch and a folding chair, but she had a fully furnished apartment.

There was a leather couch with a matching chair in the living room. In the center of the room was a coffee table, complete with a hearty cactus plant.

A stand with a decent TV sat against the wall. She now had a kitchen table and even a real bed. This family was amazing.

She'd gone upstairs to at least thank Christian, figuring he had some part in it, but he wasn't home. How was she supposed to thank this family?

Perhaps she'd see them all at the fundraiser on Saturday.

A few hours later, after having had her first real meal in her new home, she heard the door close upstairs.

With fresh cups of coffee in her hands, one for her and one for Christian, she started up the outside steps to his door.

Once she was there, with both hands full, she decided the only way to knock was with her foot. She gently kicked the back door.

Christian must have been upstairs by the time she knocked

because she could hear him stomp downstairs and through the kitchen. When he flung the door open, he was standing there in nothing but a towel, which thankfully was wrapped around his waist.

Her mouth went dry and she tried to swallow, but it only choked her instead.

When she could, she looked up into his eyes and smiled. "I was being neighborly and brought by a cup of coffee. But I can see you're very busy, so I'll…"

"Come in. I'll only be three minutes."

She stepped into the house, and he closed the door behind her.

"Have a seat." He pointed to the kitchen table.

Christian hurried away, and Darcy sat at the table. This wasn't really what she'd had in mind when she wanted to say thank you to his family. But he was comfortable, and so she sat and waited.

He was right. He'd only needed three minutes, and he was showered, dressed, and seated in front of her.

"I hope it's still hot. I could go get a fresh one," she said as he lifted the mug to his lips.

"It's good." He took a sip. "Ah, you're a weak coffee drinker, huh?"

"Weak?"

"More like tea than coffee. But good."

She nodded. Her own father used to say that, didn't he? Well, the man she'd grown up thinking was her father.

Her shoulders dropped as she thought about the deceit. She hadn't been furious since she'd found out about it, but being around the Kellers made her angry about her situation. She missed her mother and she loved her father, but why had someone given her up and not given her a family like the one she was being taken in by? An only child of two aging parents wasn't the same as what the Kellers had.

She sipped her coffee again. There was no need to get worked up. She had a perfectly good life. There was just a lot of red tape around it.

"So, why did you really come up here? You look a bit out of sorts," Christian said.

Darcy snapped her head up. "Oh, I'm sorry. Lot on my mind. But I did want to come and thank you all for the furniture. As you're the only Keller around, I thought I'd start with you."

He laughed. "Really I had nothing to do with that. I let them in the house. John, Arianna, and Regan did the rest."

"I'll have to thank them too then."

"Do you have plans Saturday night? I happen to know where they will all be."

She smiled at him. "As a matter of fact, I do have plans."

"Oh." His eyebrows drew together as he took a sip of his coffee. "I need a date and was going to ask you."

"To Simone's fundraiser?"

He looked up at her. "You sure do know your stuff."

She laughed. "I've already been invited. I will be accompanying..."

"He moves fast."

"To be honest, I think I'm going as an employee, not as a date. He was a little uncomfortable going, and he's really bad at asking."

"No kidding." Christian leaned in closer to her. "I told you he had a soft spot for you."

Her jaw tensed.

Christian sat back. "But that really kills my plans. I was hoping to ask you to go. Now I have to find a date or go stag."

"You could go with us."

He laughed. "Third wheel was never my style."

CHAPTER 11

$\mathcal{E}$d liked sushi, but this crap from the grocery store was not what he'd call sushi. But it was going to have to do. He'd sent Darcy to a build to meet the foreman and help him get organized. If anything, Darcy McCary was the most organized woman he'd ever met, next to his Aunt Regan.

When he thought about it, there were a lot of similarities between the women. Not only did they have a similar look, but just the way they did things. They both made weak coffee, though he hadn't told Darcy to alter it—not yet. They both were irritatingly tidy, and crazy efficient.

In less than a week, Darcy had nearly organized Ed's entire office, and every report he had stacked on his desk was now filed. All he had to do was say, "Darcy, where are we on..." and she knew.

His Aunt Regan had literally fallen into his Uncle Zach's lap on a bus. Well, Darcy McCary had bumped into him at a Starbucks.

The thought sent heat rising to his forehead, and he broke out into a sweat. There was no need to keep thinking about her in terms of comparing her to his aunt. They worked together, and that was where it was going to stay—a working relationship.

They might have plans for Saturday night, but that was a business arrangement. He hated fundraisers, but the work his aunt Simone did with her foundation was amazing. There was no way he'd miss it and not give her the support she deserved. But now he was dragging Darcy with him. Maybe he should tell her he'd be late and pawn her off on his brother.

Another wave of heat burst through him, and this time he reached for a tissue to wipe his face.

He'd be damned if he pushed Darcy in Christian's direction. He'd seen his brother's eyes when he'd brought her in that day. And why had he done that? Why was he being all neighborly and offering her rides in the morning so early?

Oh, that had him twisted inside. Darcy McCary was his assistant and off limits to his brother.

Ed shook his head. Dear Lord, he was losing his mind.

Why should he care if Darcy and Christian hooked up? He didn't date women in the office. Christian was a good guy. But the thought gnawed at him until he finally threw the last three pieces of the crappy sushi in the trash and headed out of his office and to the break room to find a bottle of water—of which he wasn't so sure wouldn't be better used just being poured on his head.

Later that afternoon when Darcy returned, Ed found himself in a foul mood. The moment he heard her desk drawer, he was snapping at her to come into his office.

When she walked through the door, she had a quirky smile on her face. What could that be about?

"Did you get Davenport in line then?"

She nodded. "He's a mess of a man, but he knew his stuff. I think he had coffee stains on every purchase order and a chocolate donut stain on every blue print, but he's set to go now."

Ed pursed his lips. "I guess you'll be heading home now."

She raised an eyebrow. "I have an hour left. Besides the bus I ride doesn't pick up until five-thirty. Did you have a project you needed me to start?"

No, and he wasn't sure why it had even been mentioned. He was too protective of this woman. Damn, he should have let her suffer with the ruined blouse and just hired a temp.

"No. I think I just ate some bad sushi for lunch, and now I'm irritable. Or maybe I'm hungry since I threw it away."

Darcy nodded. "Would you like me to go down to the deli and get you something decent to eat?"

He shook his head. "No, but would you mind me giving you a ride home and maybe we could stop for dinner along the way?"

Darcy crossed her arms. "I've worked for you almost a week, and you've fed me multiple times, found me a house, filled it with furniture, asked me to be your companion at a fundraiser, and now want to take me to dinner again. Did I fall into the best job, or are you one of those lonely men who only keep company with people they employ?"

Well, that made him sound horrible. "I just thought…"

"I know. I'm a little testy when it comes to being taken care of. Sorry. I was raised to fend for yourself and make things happen. This has been a bit too easy, I suppose."

"It's your first week. I'll be an ass on Monday."

She laughed. "Maybe I should keep my mouth shut then."

"So dinner?"

"I think that would be very nice. And thank you." She turned to leave as her cell phone chimed with a text message. She looked at it and laughed.

"Tell me someone sent you a funny joke. I could use a laugh."

She shifted her eyes to him under a hood of dark lashes and smiled. "It was your brother. He said I got a package, and he'd have it at his place. And this time he promises to have clothes on while I'm there."

Darcy walked out of the office smiling. Ed, on the other hand, felt the heat, which had flustered him before, now creep around his collar.

He loosened his tie and unfastened the top buttons of his shirt.

It was a good thing he was taking her home. He had a few words for his little brother.

CHAPTER 12

At five o'clock, Darcy opened his office door. "I didn't know if you were ready to go or not."

Ed shook his head. "I just got news of a delay. I'm on the phone with Valerie."

"Her company has another delay?'

"No. She's pulling us out of a pinch. One day you're the guy with your head on the chopping block. The next you're the savior."

He sat back in his chair with the phone to his ear.

Darcy checked her watch. "Unless you need me, and I'm happy to stay, why don't I get downstairs and catch that bus."

"Oh, yeah. I'm sorry. I'll be a bit, so that would be good. Valerie is headed over to help me out with this, so you're good. Have a nice night."

Darcy nodded and let herself out of the office.

Ed replaced the phone receiver and buried his face in his hands. He'd had the last hour to evaluate his earlier thoughts, and he'd decided the last thing he needed was to worry about Darcy. Starting now, he needed to put up a wall that divided his feelings. There was no place in business for feelings.

His cell phone chimed, and he looked at his text message. It was from Valerie.

I'll meet you at Steve's in twenty. TY for the invite.

At least he hadn't lied—not completely.

DARCY PULLED HER PREPACKAGED MEAL OUT OF THE MICROWAVE and set it on the counter. She could hear the opening credits to *You've Got Mail* on the television, and she hurried to pour herself a drink.

She'd been looking forward to having dinner with Ed, but now that he was "working late," she'd lose herself in her favorite movie and a manufactured meal. After all, Tom Hanks and Meg Ryan could fix anyone's bland mood.

Darcy had seen the movie so many times that she could quote every line. The movie had been one of her mother's favorites. When she was undergoing chemotherapy, they'd watched it all the time.

The purpose of the movie was to get her mind off her boss. She'd had that nasty ping of jealousy creep into her when he'd mentioned Valerie. There was no reason to worry about him with another woman. This man was her boss, and was much older than she was.

The moment Greg Kinnear's character mentioned sushi in the movie, Darcy set her food down and kicked her feet up onto the coffee table. Why did she care that Ed had thrown out his sushi and was hungry today? She'd wanted to get him a meal—and then he'd asked her to join him for one.

She was much too comfortable with him already. That was supposed to be good for a working relationship, but at the same time, he crossed her mind a bit too much.

Midway through her movie, just as Meg Ryan's character was dissing Tom Hanks's character in a news interview, there was a knock on the door.

Darcy's mind went straight to Ed. Maybe he'd come by to discuss something. Well, that would be silly—but maybe.

When she opened the door, she smiled wide. The face was close, but this one belonged to Christian.

"I need a favor."

She laughed, looking him over. He was covered from head to toe in mud, and he carried a grocery bag full of clothes. "I can't wait to hear it."

"I need to borrow your shower."

"I thought you were going to start wearing clothes around me."

"Yeah." He looked down at himself. "Charity game for a school. Sprinklers. It was a mess."

"And why are you wanting to shower down here?"

"My shower head broke. John will fix it tomorrow, but I need a shower now."

Darcy stepped back and swept her arm through the air as if to say "you know the way."

A few moments later, she heard the shower start. She picked up her half-eaten dinner and threw it in the trash. She opened two beers, which John had put in her refrigerator when he'd delivered the furniture. She set one beer on the table and took a sip from the other just as there was another knock on the door.

Again, she wondered how she had so many visitors when she didn't know anyone in this town.

She'd thought Christian standing at the door covered in mud was shocking enough, but seeing Ed standing on her doorstep, a bag from Steve's Barbecue Pit and Beer in his hands, definitely took her by surprise.

"I thought you might be hungry. I promised you dinner." He held the bag up.

"You really didn't have to do that. But I am hungry. The microwave dinner I made didn't cut it." She stepped back. "Come in."

Ed walked through the door, and the smoky smell from the restaurant lingered on him.

"I assume you ate then?" she said, taking the bag and walking to the kitchen.

"Yeah, well, sort of. Valerie was a bit preoccupied for conversation. So she scarfed her dinner and ditched me. But we got the delay figured out."

"Well, that's good. Can I offer you a beer?"

"I'd like that."

Darcy walked to the kitchen, pulled a beer out of the refrigerator, and handed it to him.

"Thanks. Are you having one?"

"I have one out here. I was just watching a movie." She walked out into the living room to fetch her beer, and he followed.

"You have another beer out. You're either having a fun evening, or..." He stopped and looked around. "Is that your shower? I caught you at a bad time."

That was when the shower turned off, and the door opened slightly letting the steam out.

"Darcy, do you have a clean towel I can use?"

"Under the sink," she said as she looked at Ed whose eyes had grown wide.

"I did interrupt."

She saw the pulse in his temple beat, and she shook her head. "No. No."

A moment later, the door opened and Christian walked out of the bathroom, only a towel wrapped around his waist.

"Hey, bro," Christian said casually.

"Don't hey bro me. What's going on here?"

Darcy stepped forward. "Nothing is going on here. He..."

"Chill out," Christian reached for the clothes he'd left on the chair. "God, you're such a freak about things."

"You're standing in her apartment in a damn towel. What am I supposed to think?"

"And what does it matter?" Christian stepped up to his brother. "She's a grown woman, and you're only her boss. Would it matter if I were here for any other reason?"

Darcy watched the two of them as they went at each other with their words.

"Christian, don't push me."

"I didn't do anything. Christ, my shower is broken. John can't fix it until tomorrow."

Ed nodded. "Oh."

"Besides, you owe her an apology for the way you just accused her without asking her calmly if something was going on. You came in here acting all bossy like you always do when you're not in control of a situation."

Christian headed back toward the bathroom.

Ed tucked his free hand into his front pocket and rocked back on his heels. "Hey, I'm sorry about that."

"It's okay."

"You had said he wasn't wearing clothes when he texted you and now…"

She scrunched her face up, and then she remembered. "Oh. No…he…"

"It's okay. He's right. It's none of my business."

Christian walked out of the bathroom dressed. "Thanks for the use of your shower. Sorry the ass here accused you, but I really appreciate it."

"My pleasure. I opened a beer for you."

Christian walked up to her and kissed her on the cheek.

"Oh, thanks, but I have to run. I have a hot date. Give it to Mr. Uptight. He could use it."

And with that, Christian disappeared out the door and up the stairs.

Darcy stood there for a moment before she turned back toward Ed.

He took a long pull from his beer. "How about some dinner?"

"Did you really think I was up to something with Christian?"

Ed let out a long breath and let his shoulders drop. "I'm sorry. It shouldn't be any of my business, even if you had been up to something."

"That's right. My private life isn't part of my job description, is it? I mean, you all seem to have taken me in, and you have no idea what that means to me. But if you're trying to be all big brother on me, I don't need that."

Ed nodded. "I was out of line."

Darcy crossed her arms in front of her. He was out of line. And she was mad that he'd assume she'd fall into bed with someone she'd just met. That certainly wasn't her style, and she was fairly sure, after having met most of his family, that wasn't his style either. So why were they standing there with tension in the air.

One thing her mother had taught her, in an awkward situation, a meal usually pulled things together. A smile formed on her lips. Perhaps that's why her mother was such a large lady. Food had cured many things in her life, and at this moment, perhaps it would clear the air.

CHAPTER 13

*D*arcy started toward the kitchen with Ed right behind her.

"Why are you smiling?" he asked as he set his beer on the table.

"I was just thinking about my mother. Whenever someone was upset, or something had gone badly, she always cooked a big meal. And here you and I are arguing, and we move into the kitchen to eat."

She pulled the containers of ribs, corn, and bread out of the bag.

"Do you eat here all the time? This is the second time this week I've eaten this."

Ed rubbed his hand over the back of his neck. "No. Valerie likes it there. It's her kind of place."

Darcy nodded. "I see." She pulled down two plates and began to fix them up. "So you and Valerie?"

She looked up at him, and his brows had narrowed in obvious confusion.

"Me and Valerie what?"

"Are you seeing her?"

"Val?" He let out a grunt. "Are you kidding me?"

Darcy carried the plates to the table. "She's not attractive?"

"No."

That made her laugh. "Why?"

"At some point I'm sure you'll meet her, but let me give you the run down. Six feet tall. Completely muscle. And not interested in people of my gender."

Darcy sat down and looked up at him as he waited for her response. She thought about it for a moment. "Oh! I see. So, if you're sister had gone to dinner with her…"

"She'd have made it further than I would have."

"Got it."

Ed sat down across from her. "She likes her beer, her NASCAR, bluegrass, and barbecue." He picked up a rib as if to drive a point. "I like my women a bit younger, too."

Darcy swallowed hard. "How much younger."

"Valerie is fifty."

"Oh, and you're?"

"Thirty-five."

He was younger than she'd thought. He was just so mature. Christian was much more playful. Darcy would have pegged Ed for forty-five or fifty, even if he didn't look fifty at all. That made her chuckle again, just as the thought of her mother. Quickly, she bit off a piece of meat to keep her mouth shut.

"So this fundraiser on Saturday—just how fancy do I need to dress?"

Ed bit off a piece of his rib. "Prom with some class."

"Oh." Darcy wrinkled up her nose. "I have a black cocktail dress."

"Isn't that supposed to work for any occasion?"

She chuckled. "Well, that was what I was hoping. I don't have a paycheck yet, and I have to pay rent. So…"

"Are you in need of money?"

"No, that's not what I was saying."

He nodded. "Right."

Darcy sat back in her chair and looked him over. "You're the caregiver in your family, aren't you?"

"What do you mean?"

"You want everyone happy and taken care of. You're the kind of person who would give the shirt off his back to someone who needed it, but you still expect everyone to pull their weight."

"That's how I was raised."

"Oh, I see that you were raised very well. But your brother is different. Not that he wouldn't take care of anyone, but he's more about himself and into having fun. He's a little more carefree."

Ed nodded. "You're very wise when it comes to people."

"I think I get that from my father. Doctors observe. He liked to watch people. He sees good in everyone, even those who aren't. But he'd like you. You're a hardworking man who takes care of what's his—like your family." And as soon as she'd said it, she realized she'd been included in that bundle.

Ed wiped his hands on a napkin, which had been included in the bag of food. "My uncle Curtis is a doctor. He's a lot like Christian—carefree. He sees things in people though, just like you said your dad does. I suppose that's how he ended up with Aunt Simone. He saw past the oil heiress, even when she didn't."

"So this fundraiser. What kind of organization does your aunt run?"

Ed smiled wide. "It's called the Diamond Gift." He pulled from his beer and continued. "When she first came to live in America full time, she had been cut off from her father. My uncle's friend got her a job at a clinic." He laughed. "Now, when I say she was an oil heiress, I mean lot, stock, and barrel. Diamonds, clothes, cars, you name it. She was a princess. So, when her dad kicked her to the curb, she had to find a job and learn to work."

"Why would her father do something like that?"

The grin was back, and she noticed he had a little dimple in his cheek when the grin kept a secret behind it. "She was pregnant."

"Oh. And that was unacceptable."

He shrugged. "I guess when you've gotten in trouble with some common person."

"Your family is anything but common, by the way."

There was a gleam in his eyes. "I know."

"Anyway…the organization."

He took a bite of his rib and washed it down with his beer. "One day there was this woman who was in the clinic. Her room-mate was filling up the woman's bag with diapers and formula for her kid. She'd been abused by her husband numerous times, and the people at the clinic would keep her there until they had to release her. But they took care of her. Anyway, Simone had a moment of clarity, I guess, and she took off her enormous diamond earrings and gave them to the woman to pawn. It would give her enough money to get away from her husband for at least a few days and maybe get some help."

"And the woman…"

"Kissed her and thanked her and is now the Vice President of the organization."

"You're kidding me?"

"Nope. She pawned the earrings and found a shelter. With that one gift of good fortune, given to her by Simone, who until that day was all about herself, she was able to help herself. So that's what the organization is about. Helping women get on their feet and away from those holding them back."

"That's wonderful."

"They've had some amazing successes. But with every success, there are a few failures."

"Someone who takes their generosity and takes advantage of it."

He shrugged again. "Or who goes back to an abusive relation-ship and ends up dead."

The blood drained from her head, and she searched for a napkin before he could see the tears form in her eyes. "That's horrible."

"It's reality." He pushed his plate away. "I don't understand why women get into those kinds of relationships, but even my Aunt Regan was in one before she married Uncle Zach. The man tried to kill her."

Darcy shook her head. "I don't understand either."

Ed blew out a long breath. "I suppose I should head out." He stood from the table, and Darcy followed.

"Thank you for dinner—again."

"Maybe someday we can do better than ribs."

"Maybe in a few weeks I can take you out to dinner." The moment the words were out of her mouth, she regretted them. This was her boss. She couldn't be asking him out to dinner.

He only nodded, which made her feel incredibly small.

Ed walked to the door and pulled it open. "I'll see you tomorrow."

"Yes, you will."

There was an odd silence that fell between them. That kind of silence that was usually filled with a hug—or a kiss.

Darcy gripped the door handle as Ed stood in the dark stairwell.

"Well, goodnight," his voice was soft.

"Goodnight." Hers was on the edge of breathless.

Ed lingered his stare a moment longer and finally turned and hurried up the stairs.

Darcy shut the door and locked it before leaning her back up against it. She seriously needed to reel in her feelings for this man. In that moment between them, she could have made a complete fool of herself and wrapped him up in her arms and smothered him with kisses.

Just the thought of it had her sliding down the door and sitting on the floor.

She looked around at the fully furnished apartment.

What had she fallen into?

What kind of family gives so freely?

She tucked her lips in between her teeth and bit down to keep them from trembling. It was very possible this family would lead her to the information she'd come to Tennessee for. She was now deeply embedded in the Benson, Benson, and Hart organization —but it was going to come at a cost.

One wrong move and she'd not only lose her job, but Ed was becoming very important to her.

She'd met a handful of his family already, and she was embraced by them. What if the rest of the family didn't like her? What if they did like her, but found out she was going to use Ed to find her birth parents? What if her birth parents were horrible people, and the reason she was led to Benson, Benson, and Hart was because of something bad they did and not because they just worked there?

It wasn't supposed to matter. She was just looking for information. But now...now it was personal.

A bead of sweat rolled down the back of Darcy's neck. Perhaps she'd better quickly decide which was more important— finding her birth parents or the feelings she was fighting over Ed Keller.

CHAPTER 14

$\mathcal{E}$d sank down onto his couch and sat in the dark. There was no reason, not a one, for him to have gone over to Darcy's tonight. But he'd shown up anyhow. Brought food. And then he'd accused her of doing things with his own brother.

He scrubbed his hands over his face.

It really didn't matter. Christian could ask her to marry her, and they could run off tomorrow—that should be fine. But it wasn't.

There was something about Darcy McCary that had Ed out of sorts, and nothing did that to him—nothing.

It was just circumstantial. It had been a strange week. There had been delays. And no matter how useful and good she was, Darcy was still a new employee and had needed to be trained. He'd needed someone steady to run his office for a long time, and there she was.

He'd admit, though only to himself, even though her resume was impressive, he'd given her the job because he'd felt sorry for her. His whole life he'd had family to pull him out of any situation he'd ever been in. It was obvious Darcy didn't have that. It was a benefit that she was an amazing assistant. He'd been more productive in the few days that she'd run his office than he had been in a long time.

It could be her organization, but he knew there was more.

She took care of him, and he'd been looking for someone to do that for a long time too.

The lights from a passing car illuminated the living room, but then it was dark again. Ed looked at his watch. It was getting late and he'd wanted to be in the office early tomorrow, but he couldn't shut down his mind.

He stood and walked up the stairs to his bedroom.

The bed was still unmade, and there was a pile of clothes on the floor in front of the hamper. With a huff, he picked up the clothes and threw them in the empty basket.

This wasn't the kind of keeping he'd needed. He knew that, so why was it so important to make sure Darcy was taken care of so she could take care of him?

Ed kicked off his shoes and pulled off his pants. His office keys fell from the pocket and clanked on the floor. That had been one reason he'd gone to her house, he thought as he bent to pick up the keys. He'd made her a set.

He looked at his watch again. It was much too late to go back over there. This was just something that was going to have to wait until tomorrow. Right now, Ed needed to get some rest. Preparation would start tomorrow on a proposal that could be big for BBH. It would be good to have Darcy by his side on this.

Ed shook his head. No, it would be good to get a decent night sleep and stop obsessing over his new assistant.

ED LOOKED UP FROM HIS DESK AS HIS UNCLE WALKED THROUGH THE door.

"Your assistant's desk is very tidy," he said on a laugh as he crossed the room and sat in a chair in front of Ed's desk.

"She's very efficient. Thank goodness."

"Heard you ran her over in a Starbucks."

Ed shook his head. "She ran into me. My luck."

"I suppose so." Zach looked down at his phone and grinned. "Had a woman fall into my lap on a bus once. Just my luck."

Ed leaned back in his chair. "Is that why you're in here? You've come to tease me over the similarities?"

Zach chuckled. "It's just funny how things happen."

"I suppose."

It was then he could hear the familiar noise of the desk drawer opening just beyond his office door. A moment later, he could smell her perfume.

"Darcy?" he called out. "Come on in here when you get a moment."

Zach leaned in toward the desk and whispered, "You sound bossy."

Ed let out a groan when his uncle laughed under his breath and sat back in his chair.

A moment later, Darcy walked through the door, a legal notepad already in her hand—just in case.

"Darcy, I wanted you to meet my uncle Zach."

Darcy walked fully into the office as Zach stood up and turned to meet her.

She held out her hand. "It's a pleasure to meet you, sir."

But Zach's reaction wasn't what Ed had expected. He'd expected professional. He'd expected an easy smile, a joke, a comforting word to her at Ed's expense.

Zach's mouth had actually fallen open as he shook the woman's hand. "Darcy, it's nice to meet you. I've heard a lot about you."

"Likewise. I've met a great deal of your family already, and I just want to thank you all for your generosity."

Zach nodded, still keeping Darcy's hand in his.

She glanced at Ed and then back to Zach. "Is everything okay? I didn't interrupt, did I?"

Zach shook his head. "No. Not at all." His voice had lightened. "It's just that you look so familiar to me. Where are you from?"

"Kentucky. I just came to Nashville a few weeks ago to try out the big city."

"Well, I'm glad you're here to take care of this slob." Now that was more like it, Ed thought.

"He doesn't give me too much trouble."

Zach leaned in closer to her. "Yet. But my money is on you."

Ed stood from his seat. "Okay, I'm sure you have a meeting to get ready for, and I have to prep Darcy for it."

Zach laughed and finally let go of Darcy's hand. "I'll see you in the conference room in an hour."

Zach walked out of the office, whistling a tune.

Ed wrinkled up his nose. "Sorry. I don't know what came over him."

"No worries. So tell me about this meeting."

Darcy listened as Ed went over what would happen in the meeting they were headed to, but her mind kept wandering to Zach's reaction when he'd seen her. It might have been a genuine reaction of mistaken identity, but then again, maybe it wasn't.

Zach was an original fixture at BBH. He'd have known everyone that came through the door. Even if it had been before he'd taken over, he was still ingrained in the makings of the company.

Uncle Zach was about to become Darcy's best friend.

CHAPTER 15

$\mathcal{D}$arcy had been briefed on the meeting they were about to attend. It was the first time she'd seen Charlie since she started, and it gave her some satisfaction to see the busty blonde take the cold shoulder from Ed. With the exception of Zach Benson, the other men were having a hard time focusing.

The meeting had already started when another woman walked through the door, quietly as if not to disrupt. She carried a notebook and tucked herself into a chair at the right of Zach.

Business went on as normal, and the woman simply melded in.

Darcy did her best to keep track of numbers and lists, but Zach Benson's reaction to her still had her itching for more information.

During the meeting, Zach would often lean in to the woman who had sat down next to him. There was great comfort between them, but by Ed's reaction when she'd walked into the room, this wasn't his aunt. Perhaps this was his uncle's assistant, whom she hadn't met yet. The woman was in her late fifties, at least. When Zach would quietly make a comment to her, it was returned with a nod and a note written on the pad.

Comfort between two, like she was seeing, was something built over time. Zach and his assistant had a history.

It was then Darcy's mind began to spin. What kind of history did they have? Had they simply worked together for a very long time—or was there a secret buried between them?

Darcy's hands began to shake. As she bore down on her pen to make a note, she pressed to hard and broke the tip off the pen. Blue ink instantly pooled on the paper she'd been diligently keeping notes on.

All eyes were on her, and the woman to Zach's side was quick to grab a stack of napkins from the coffee credenza and head her way.

"That isn't the first time I've see that happen," the woman said as she scooped the pen out of Darcy's hands and quickly disposed of it with minimal damage from dripping ink.

She gave Darcy a napkin for her hands and then retrieved another notepad from a cabinet in the corner. With a quick smile she was back, sitting next to Zach, and the meeting continued.

Darcy could feel the sting of tears threatening to let loose, but this wasn't the place to lose her composure. Accidents happened, though she'd had her fair share this week.

Ed leaned over to her and pushed his engraved pen toward her. "Here, this one will hold up."

Darcy pursed her lips and took the pen. "Thank you."

Ed touched her hand and then retracted his, quickly but calmly, as if it was second nature to touch someone so gently in a meeting. No one had noticed the exchange, but it had done a number on Darcy's insides.

She willed her heart to stop pounding and her breath to slow. Lord, she hoped she wasn't sweating.

Busting open a pen during an important meeting had been bad enough, but this giddy feeling she got when Ed touched her was ridiculous.

Could she be so in need of personal attention that the

slightest caring reaction from her boss could keep sending her into shock?

"Okay, I like how this is all laying out. Let's break for lunch and meet back here at two," Zach announced as he stood from his chair.

Darcy gathered her notes and the ruined pad, as well. Perhaps she could decipher what had been written before her mind caused her to make a fool of herself.

Ed gently touched her shoulder. "I'm going to run down to the deli and get us some lunch. I want to go over some other projects before we have to be back in here. Do you like pastrami?"

The amount of information buzzing in her head was a bit overwhelming. She'd have liked to have sat out by the river for a bit and calm down, but she only nodded at Ed's offer.

"Great. I'll be back up in a half hour."

As he hurried away, the woman who had helped her clean up her mess was walking toward her. They were the only two left in the large room.

Darcy tried to compose herself, and she could only hope she looked half as professional as the woman walking toward her.

"You must be Darcy. I've been hearing good things about you." The woman stuck out her hand. "I'm Mary Ellen."

"Nice to meet you."

"I'm Mr. Benson's assistant. He couldn't do anything without me," she said on a laugh, and Darcy choked one out as well, realizing the woman was trying to keep the mood light.

"Thank you for coming to my rescue."

"Oh, I've had that happen to me a million times. I blame it on the shoddy manufacturing of your basic stick pen, but really, sometimes these meetings get so bogged down with number writing that my hand just crushes the pen."

Darcy laughed again. Whoever this woman was—aside from Zach Benson's assistant—she was easy to like.

"Why don't you come up with me, and we'll type these notes up quickly. I know you probably can't read too much of what's left on your page."

Darcy looked down at the paper that now looked like kinder-garten art. "Thank you."

They both gathered their things, and Darcy followed Mary Ellen out of the office. Her desk was only around the corner, and she set her notebook down and pulled an extra chair around the desk for Darcy.

"Have a seat. It won't take me long to type these up. Besides, while Zach works out, I'll have someone to talk to."

"He works out during the day?"

Mary Ellen nodded as she began to type the notes into the computer. "It keeps him focused. If you saw his office, you'd think it was a small apartment. All the luxuries of home."

It was time to ease this woman into some conversation. "You seem very comfortable with Mr. Benson."

"I should be. I've been with him since he took over that desk."

Mary Ellen was going to be a great asset, too.

Darcy looked around the office. It had quieted down. Everyone must be at lunch. She took a deep breath and crossed her legs, trying her best to act casual.

"So how long have you been his assistant?"

Mary Ellen shot her a sideways glance and then focused back on her computer screen. "Isn't that like asking a woman her age?"

Darcy felt the blood drain from her face. "I didn't mean any disrespect."

Mary Ellen laughed. "I'm just kidding." She flipped over her notes and continued to type. "Let's see, I started when I was fresh out of junior college. I was with him for ten years before I hired his wife."

"You hired his wife?"

Mary Ellen nodded. "I needed to replace myself as his

assistant. Seems like such a long time ago. I was pregnant and desperate to leave him in good hands."

As Mary Ellen finished typing up the notes, Darcy rubbed her palms against her skirt. Why was it that Zach Benson had looked at Darcy the way he had? And why was he so comfortable with Mary Ellen?

Her mouth went dry.

Could it have been this simple? Had fate thrown her into Ed Keller so that she'd get the job at Benson, Benson, and Hart? She'd expected it to take years before she found the people who gave her away. But, as she sat beside the woman who had quickly come to her aid, she began to wonder—were Zach Benson and his assistant her birth parents? Had they hid their secret all these years and now here she was?

Darcy thought she just might get sick.

CHAPTER 16

*E*d watched as Darcy pulled meat off her bread, set it to the side, and then rebuild her sandwich. Just a little persnickety, he thought, until she started the process over.

This time he reached for her hand and stopped her. "Is there something on your mind? I bought the sandwich hoping you'd eat it."

Darcy looked down at the food as if she hadn't noticed. "I'm sorry."

"You don't have to apologize. You don't look so well."

"I'm very sorry. I have something on my mind, and I just can't get it to go away."

When Ed had set the sandwiches on the boardroom table, he'd taken the seat right next to her. It hadn't been thought out. It had just happened. But he found himself scooting his chair over so he could be close enough to her to touch her in some comforting way.

He rested his arm around her shoulders. "Everything's all right though? Your dad, he's okay?"

"Yes."

"You're homesick?"

Darcy dropped her shoulders, and Ed pulled his arm away.

"Maybe." She picked up a napkin and wiped her eyes. "I don't want to talk about it. Not now." She reassembled her sandwich. "I'll be fine by the time we start the meeting back up."

"You're keeping up okay?"

"Minus the pen catastrophe, I'm doing great."

Ed laughed. "Stupid stick pens."

THEY'D CLEANED UP THEIR LUNCH, AND DARCY WENT BACK TO HER desk to attend to the pile Ed had started for her. She decided it was a good thing that she was single and no one would be waiting for her at home. It looked as though the more competent in her job she became, the more work Eduardo Keller had for her.

The pile on her desk hadn't dwindled too far when Ed came walking back into the office carrying a small bag. She honestly hadn't noticed he wasn't even in his office.

"Zach wants to discuss a project in Georgia before we start the meeting up. So, if you don't mind, we need to head down to the boardroom."

"Not a problem," she said as she reached for her notepad.

She opened her top desk drawer to search for a new pen. That was when Ed set the bag he carried on the top of the desk.

"Try this one," he said.

The bag was a small, white bag with rope handles. Tissue paper stuck out from the top.

Darcy bit down on her lip, trying to keep her emotions in check. For all she knew, there was one of those spring coiled snakes in the bag that would jump out at her.

She reached inside and pulled out a box. When she lifted the lid, she found an engraved pen set.

DARCY MCCARY

94

She swallowed the lump in her throat. "You had these made for me?"

Ed shrugged his shoulders. "You looked like you could use a pick me up. And a useful one at that."

Darcy sat back in her chair and looked up at the man whose dark eyes looked back at her.

"Thank you."

"You're welcome. Now grab your pad and one of those pens, and let's go. He's waiting."

Darcy nodded and did just as he'd said, but as she followed him back to the boardroom, her knees began to shake. Perhaps she should stop all the silly thoughts she had about finding her birth parents. It was going to get in the way of her job. And her job was getting in the way of her feelings for Eduardo Keller— she was very sure she was falling for the man.

THE MEETING HAD GONE ON FOR ANOTHER THREE HOURS. DARCY had missed her first bus, and now she waited for another.

She'd had three people ask if she needed a ride, and she'd turned them all down. Of course they'd been Ed, Zach, and Mary Ellen—and right now, all three of them were making her brain hurt. Ed most of all.

The generosity of this man was beyond anything she'd ever known. There was going to be a breaking point—there had to be.

Why was it he never hired anyone and only used temps? Was it because they didn't work well when he fed them and gave them gifts? Or was this more?

Did he over work his temps and they quit? Was he just buttering her up and soon the whole world would shut down around her, and she'd be forced into hard work like she'd never known?

As the bus pulled up, Darcy hoisted her purse up on her shoulder and pulled the money she'd readied out of her pocket.

Tomorrow night was the fundraiser, and she'd agreed to go with Ed. It would certainly prove to be an interesting venture. She'd take it for what it was worth. A working evening—in a cocktail dress.

No doubt she'd be there with Zach and his wife. She wondered if Mary Ellen would be there too?

As the bus bounced through town, she wondered how much Zach's wife knew about Mary Ellen. She'd been the one to hire her—Regan, right?—but then Ed had said Zach had fired her.

Darcy's head was spinning.

Only something so twisted could mean that things had happened. Why would someone fire their own wife? And why had Zach looked at her the way he had?

The more she got to thinking of it, Christian had looked at her that way too—with curious eyes as though they'd met.

Darcy clenched her purse in her arms. This was stupid. Hadn't she been told a million times during her lifetime that she looked like someone's cousin?

That's when the sinking feeling hit her stomach. She had been told that a million times, only she didn't know it was possible. She hadn't known she'd been adopted.

Someone had hit the signal for the bus to stop, and when Darcy looked up, she realized it was her stop as well.

She stood and filed off the bus when the doors opened.

As she walked up the sidewalk, Christian backed out of the driveway. He rolled down his window and rested his arm on the door.

"Hey, it's my beautiful housemate."

She smiled. "Thank you for the compliment."

"A package came for you today. I set it by your door. A package from home."

"Thanks." She noticed he was dressed up and not wearing anything athletic. "You going out?"

"Yeah. The sister of one of my teammate's wives." He rolled

his eyes. "But, at least if this goes good, I can drag her to that fundraising event tomorrow night—unless you've reconsidered and would rather go with me than my brother."

Darcy laughed. "I'm just using him to climb the corporate ladder."

This time, Christian laughed. "I think you're already doing that. You got permanent employee status, not temp status."

Hadn't she already found that odd?

She gave him a wave. "Have a good night."

Christian held up his hand and crossed his fingers. Then he gave her a wave and backed out of the driveway and headed down the street.

The package Christian had said was by her door was waiting for her. She recognized her father's handwriting immediately.

The anticipation of opening it reminded her of Christmas morning. How her mother would make her hold all her gifts on her lap while she took a picture.

She held the package to her chest.

She missed her mother.

Darcy opened the door to her apartment and walked inside. She sat down on the couch and held tight to the box. She'd been mad for so long over finding out she was adopted and then over her mother's quick illness and death. But having met some of the Kellers had made her miss what she'd had. And, though it had been small, it had been her family.

Darcy opened the package and pulled out the contents. Her father had added family pictures, college transcripts, and important papers—such as her birth certificate.

She let out a slow, steady breath. She'd asked her father for the items before she'd secured the job with Benson, Benson, and Hart. The pictures had been a bonus and would look wonderful on her walls.

As she held the birth certificate in her fingers, she thought about what a lie it was.

Her parents' names were on that piece of paper, but they hadn't given birth to her. Someone else did, and she wanted to know who.

She ran her hands over her face. Why was she obsessing over this? Her parents loved her, and that should be enough. But didn't every adopted child want to know why they were given up, and by who?

How would she know? She was the only person she'd ever known who was adopted. And wouldn't that have been nice to have known as she was growing up.

Darcy ran her fingers over the print on the official document. Born at Nashville General Hospital.

She sat back on the couch. She'd come full circle to where her life started. Now the man she had feelings for was imbedded in the company that her investigator had sent her to because someone there had something to do with her.

She squeezed her eyes shut.

Were there two people at Benson, Benson, and Hart who held a secret—her secret?

CHAPTER 17

Time had slipped away, again, and Ed sat in his office staring out over the river as the sun went down.

The build in Georgia was going to be extensive. The proposal they'd worked on all day would be right there in Nashville. And he had to admit, to himself, that it was going to be a delight to have Darcy there. In the week they'd worked together, she had organized everything.

Of course, there was the obvious as well...she'd done a job on him.

Ed loosened his tie and pulled it off. He laid it on the desk. He looked up when he heard a tapping on the door. Zach stood there, his own tie loose around his neck and his suit coat draped over his arm.

"Your aunt would like to invite you to dinner."

"Is she cooking?"

Zach laughed. "She hasn't done much of that since the boys moved away from home. Either she's living large or is in denial."

Ed smiled. "I think that would be nice."

"Darcy already left for the night?"

"Yes. She'll be sleeping at her desk soon enough, especially with the Georgia and Nashville builds."

"You know," he smiled, "your aunt and I did a lot of late nights and trips away from the office."

Ed bit down on the inside of her cheek. "You assume I hired Darcy for something other than her ability to run my office."

"No. I just think there is more there than her being just an assistant."

That was something he didn't want to be obvious. He was having a hard enough time with that himself.

"I don't think that would be a very good idea."

"You can't help fate. I mean, she did run right into you, right?"

"That doesn't mean history is going to repeat itself."

Zach shrugged. "You never know." He turned to leave. "I'll meet you downstairs."

It was late when Ed got home, and all he wanted to do was climb into bed.

Dinner with Regan and Zach Benson was always a treat, and Ed appreciated it when they spent time with him. Zach had become a very important person in his life at just the right time—a role model. He hoped that he'd been a role model for their children.

Regan had wanted to hear, first hand, about the new assistant. She was a bit too thrilled that he'd "bumped into her" and then hired her.

Ed hoped he hadn't given her any reaction when she began planning a future for him and Darcy. The truth was, though he'd had an undeniable attraction to her, he knew it would wean off. If he'd been able to keep a woman, he'd be married. But Ed Keller was all about his job, and that left very little time for anything else.

His mother had said that the right woman just hadn't come

around yet. His father said he was doing the right thing by holding off. Zach had been something like forty by the time he'd gotten married, and Ed thought he still was quite a vibrant man in his sixties. Of course, age had never been an issue with Ed. He'd been a hard worker and had climbed the corporate ladder, rung by rung. He was already seated in the V.P. chair by the time anyone knew he was Zach's nephew. There was nothing anyone could say. He'd started at the very bottom. In fact, he owed as much of his success in life to his uncle John for letting him get his hands dirty on a lot of projects that no one else would take on.

He could plan out the greatest builds and help build skyscrapers from drawing to grand opening. He had all the tools. There wasn't a job on the site that Ed Keller hadn't done himself.

That's what had humored Regan the most. How could Ed do every job in an organization as big as Benson, Benson, and Hart and not be able to find a girl? But one had bumped right into him, and he'd hired her. That was an act of commitment right there. If Ed couldn't make life work so that he'd have a little love in there, his aunt figured the next best thing would be for it to just "happen" along—and it had.

But Ed didn't want those kinds of complications in the workplace. He didn't fancy dating his assistant. For one, if they dated and things didn't work out, then he was back in the same boat he was in a week ago. And on the other hand, if they did work out, it would be awkward and again he'd end up back where he was a week ago when Darcy decided to go home and raise babies.

Ed fixed his pillows, laced his hands under his head, and laid back.

He'd gone too far with that last thought. Babies.

Tomorrow would certainly be a challenge. His entire family would be at that fundraiser. Each and every one of them knew how he met Darcy, and it must have been just a little obvious that there were sparks between them. Well, sparks could be extinguished as well as a blazing fire.

Ed shifted in his bed to get comfortable. A plan brewed in his head.

Distance. That's what he needed from Darcy—distance.

He'd send the car for her tomorrow. Christian would be at the fundraiser, and Darcy McCary was plenty comfortable with his brother, though that piece of information clawed at him. But, if he was going to keep some space between them, this would be the perfect opportunity.

Yes, if he didn't show up to the fundraiser with Darcy on his arm, and she came as only an employee—alone, they'd all have to leave alone this silly notion of fate happening again.

CHAPTER 18

*D*arcy looked in the mirror and smiled. The black cocktail dress she'd brought with her to Tennessee looked nice. She'd gone out and bought a new pair of high heels, using the money her father had sent her, as well as a pair of cheap, but fancy earrings.

Her hair was pulled back to the base of her neck and rolled into a low bun. This showed off the earrings even better.

By all accounts, she figured she was ready for the evening with the Keller family—and Ed.

Butterflies fought for space in her stomach. Certainly they wouldn't stay all night. At some point, it would all ease.

This time the knock at the door was expected. However, when she opened it and only the driver was there—that part was not expected.

"Mr. Keller has sent me to take you to the fundraiser."

"Oh, and is he in the car?"

"No, Ma'am. He will not be joining us this evening."

Darcy felt her jaw click she'd clenched it so tightly. He wasn't going to go? Was this some kind of joke?

The thought raced through her mind that she wasn't going

either then. Why do this alone? This wasn't her family, or her organization, or...

She looked around the small apartment as she turned to pick up her purse and her shawl. The house had furniture. Her kitchen had been stocked. Most of all, she had a place to live.

Ed Keller might have done some of that, but the Keller family did the rest. She needed to go and thank them.

Darcy sucked in a deep breath of courage and turned to leave with the driver.

DARCY TRIED TO PAY ATTENTION TO WHERE SHE WAS BEING TAKEN. The single-woman-in-a-big-city sense took over when she realized she was at the mercy of the driver.

It shouldn't have surprised her when he turned into the Gaylord Opryland Hotel. When the driver opened the door for her to exit the car, another man was there to escort her into the Victorian Theater.

As they approached, she could hear the live music flow from the room, which was already filled with people.

Those butterflies in her stomach must have multiplied. But she'd been taught by her mother to take control of a room by walking into it with your head held high—no matter what your insides were doing.

Darcy lifted her chin, tucked her purse under her arm, and walked through the doors.

She looked around the room for someone who was familiar to her. After all, she knew some of the Kellers. At least one of them had to be there, right?

"Darcy, you look beautiful."

She recognized the voice. When she turned, there stood Christian holding two flutes of champagne.

"Christian, it's nice to see you dressed," she laughed.

"But admit it. I rock a towel."

She felt the heat rise in her cheeks.

He nodded his head to the waiter carrying another tray of champagne flutes. The man turned back to them, and Darcy took one from the tray.

"Where's your date?" Christian asked.

Darcy forced a smile. "The driver picked me up and said Mr. Keller wouldn't be joining us this evening."

"He what?" Christian's brows drew together and his lips pursed.

It was obvious Ed had still been expected.

"Well, you certainly won't be alone. C'mon."

Darcy followed Christian through the crowd of people to a table near the dance floor and stage. The table was nearly full, and she assumed this was the Keller family. Immediately she recognized John and Arianna. Zach sat next to John, but there was an empty chair to his side.

"Everyone, I want you to meet Darcy, Ed's loyal assistant," he announced and then added, under his breath, "Though he doesn't deserve it." Everyone stood up. Christian set his drink on the table and handed the other to a blonde woman to his right.

"Darcy, let me introduce you around." He took her arm and began to lead her around the table. "My father, Carlos. My mother, Madeline." Each of them shook her hand and greeted her. "My grandparents, Emily and Allen Keller."

He'd been right. They didn't look to be in their nineties, but when they passed, she did hear his grandfather ask who she was.

"This is my Uncle Curtis and his daughter, Avery."

Curtis took her hand and narrowed his eyes. "Zach's right. You do look familiar. Maybe that was why Ed was so comfortable to hire you. Welcome to our event."

She thought if he were so comfortable, he'd have shown up.

Christian continued around the table. "This is Spencer and Tyler."

Each of the men shook her hand, and an odd sensation ran

through her arm as she touched each of them. It was her turn to notice the familiarity in the boys.

"These are Zach's sons."

She felt a lump form in her throat, and it threatened to choke her. Zach. Her thoughts of earlier zipped through her mind. Mary Ellen and Zach.

The world was beginning to spin.

If Zach was, in fact, hiding his paternity of her, and Mary Ellen had given her up for adoption, then that would mean these were her brothers.

"It's very nice to meet you both."

Tyler held her hand a moment longer. "Are you all right? Your hand is shaking."

"Just a bit overwhelmed, I think."

"We get that a lot. This is one large and eclectic group."

As they continued around the table, both John and Arianna stood and greeted her with a hug.

Arianna bent to whisper in her ear. "He got cold feet?"

"I'm sure something came up, and he got busy."

Arianna let out a grunt.

Zach held out his hand to shake hers, but then pulled her in for a hug. "You sure do fit in here, don't you?" He stepped back and looked her over. "You look very nice this evening."

"Thank you, sir."

"No need to be so formal." He lifted his head as someone approached. "Oh, here's a very important part of my team."

Darcy turned her head to see Mary Ellen walking toward them. She waved and smiled. Zach's lips had turned up into proud grin, and Darcy's stomach turned.

Mary Ellen gave her a big hug. "Oh, I'm so glad you're here. Simone throws the very best parties. I suppose that's why she makes so much money off of these events for her charity." Mary Ellen looked around. "Ed?"

"Wasn't able to make it."

"Is that a fact? Well, I'm glad you're here. Remind me later to introduce you to my husband and my girls."

Darcy nodded, but inside her heart thudded in her chest. Her stomach clenched. What kind of people where these two? What they had was so casual? This was her life! They had messed with her life!

At that moment, Zach looked up again and the smile on his lips changed. "Oh, and here comes the love of my life right now."

CHAPTER 19

*W*alking toward them, through the crowd of people, was a woman whom Darcy could swear she'd seen a million times. Perhaps it was that she was a very refined version of Arianna, whom Darcy was more familiar with.

Zach pulled her into his side. "Sweetheart, this is Darcy, Ed's new assistant. Darcy, this is my wife, Regan."

Regan held her hand out to her, and her eyes grew wide. "I've heard so much about you. Welcome."

This time, not only did her hands shake, but her palms began to sweat. "It's nice to meet you, Mrs. Benson."

"Oh, please call me Regan. Zach and Ed have told me so much about you. I couldn't wait to meet you."

Darcy forced a smile. Did this woman even know the lies and deceit that ran in her small circle? This man to their side held secrets, and she probably didn't even know about them.

Their attention was diverted when a woman walked on stage. She was possibly the most beautiful woman Darcy had ever seen, and when she began to thank everyone for attending, she knew that was Simone.

Christian led Darcy back around the table to the blonde which he'd earlier handed the drink to.

"Darcy, this is my date, Victoria."

The woman remained seated, but held her hand out to shake Darcy's.

"Call me Tori. It's nice to meet you."

Christian pulled out a chair for Darcy, and she quickly sat down before her legs gave out.

Simone continued to thank everyone for attending and then introduced the entertainment.

"I am so proud of this young lady. Please help me welcome my very talented niece, Clara Keller."

The table of people around her cheered and clapped.

Christian leaned in next to her. "That's my baby sister."

She remembered that John had mentioned she was the talented one, and when she began strumming on her guitar and singing a Carrie Underwood song, Darcy wondered just how long she'd be singing at venues for her aunt. The woman was amazing.

AS THE NIGHT PROGRESSED, CLARA CONTINUED TO PERFORM, people danced, and food was served. The Kellers moved around the table, not one of them keeping a seat for very long. Each of them had included her in their conversations, and she found that she enjoyed Ed's mother tremendously. Too bad she wanted to smack Madeline Keller's son across the face the next time she saw him, but she'd never let on.

Zach and Regan had gone out to dance and so had Christian and Tori. Darcy sat and sipped her drink, but a hand on her shoulder caught her attention. She spun to see Mary Ellen standing behind her.

Darcy clenched her jaw and forced a smile as she stood.

"I wanted to introduce you to my girls. My husband is in the hall, taking a business call." The women to her side were the spitting image of the woman. They were fair complected and their hair hinted of red, where as Darcy's was very dark. Certainly, she hadn't expected them to be so similar. Well, she hadn't seen the husband yet. Perhaps they took after him, too.

The obsession with dissecting this woman's life was killing her. Darcy knew this wasn't the time or place to ask the woman the questions that burned in her head. But she would. Oh, she would.

The night went on. Christian had asked her to dance, but she had declined. She'd wanted to dance with Ed, but now she was so mad at him she figured she'd have to quit.

Regan walked around the table and sat down next to her. "Are you having fun?"

"It's been a very lovely evening."

"I'm glad. Zach tells me you and Ed literally ran into each other at Starbucks."

Darcy nodded. Under the table, she wrung the napkin in her lap with her hands. This woman made her very nervous.

"We did. My drink spilled down the front of me and ruined my interview suit."

Regan laughed easily. "I got caught in a rain storm the morning I was to start at BBH. Mary Ellen laughed when she saw me come off the elevator."

This was opening some doors. Perhaps she could maneuver her way around the conversation a bit.

"Ed said you'd met your husband on the bus?"

Regan laughed, and her eyes sparkled. "I fell into his lap. I rode to work on his lap, but I didn't know he was my new boss." She leaned in closer. "I wasn't very impressed when I found out he was."

Didn't Darcy understand that all too well?

Regan sat back. "It didn't take me long to fall in love though."

"You were his assistant?"

"Yep, until he fired me and hired Mary Ellen back."

The woman was smiling. How could she see the joy in that?

"You'd met Mary Ellen before you started?"

"She hired me. She was going on maternity leave. She'd worked for Zach for years, and she wanted someone to take good care of him."

Maternity leave. The muscles in her neck tightened.

Again, Regan laughed. "I'm sure no one had a first day like I did. She went into labor, and we had to take her to the hospital. Oh, Curtis was frantic when he saw me there." She sighed. "Babies come when they're ready, even if you're not."

Regan looked up, and Zach was motioning her to the dance floor.

"It was nice to chat with you. Looks like my man wants to take a spin." She stood and placed her hand on Darcy's shoulder. "I hope Ed keeps you around. I rather enjoy you."

She gave her a wink and then headed out with her husband.

It was time to get out of there. Darcy was very sure her time with the Kellers was about over. As soon as she had a few more bits of information, she'd demand that Mary Ellen and Zach tell her about their affair and about her birth. After all, if they were so compatible, and even now still worked so closely, why didn't they keep her?

CHAPTER 20

*D*arcy had very much done Cinderella at the ball. She'd high-tailed it out of that hall as if the dress she wore would turn into a rag.

The moment she was in her own house, she stripped off the black dress, kicked off the shoes she'd worn, and took down her hair. It was as if she needed to rid herself of the person all those people had met.

When she was done, she plopped down on her sofa in a pair of lounge pants, a Kentucky University T-shirt, and her hair pushed back in a headband. If only she'd had a pint, or even a gallon, of Ben and Jerry's, she'd be set to have the biggest pity party.

She was an idiot. She'd asked for this. It wasn't anyone else's idea to hire someone to tell her where the trail to her birth parents led. It was fate that put her in that building with the nephew of the man she was damn sure fathered her.

Without ice cream to soothe her, she turned on the TV, hoping to find some great Tom Hanks flick to take her away. He was her father's favorite actor and watching his movies always made her feel better.

No luck.

She stopped on an episode of I Love Lucy.

There was a knock at the door, and she was sure her soul jumped from her body. She was so startled she'd even thrown the remote across the room.

It was late. No one in their right mind should be knocking on her door.

Ed stood in the dark stairwell and waited for her to open the door. His nerves were shot, and the Jack and Coke he'd drank, before he'd decided to get in his car and apologize face to face, was now sitting heavy in his empty stomach.

Like a stalker, he'd sat outside her house and contemplated what he was going to say—and do.

Truth was, he'd chickened out. Every member of his family would have seen right through him. Everyone would have known he had feelings for this woman he just met.

He really should stick to women his own age, but at the moment, it seemed like the twenty-four year old Miss McCary was much more mature than he was.

The gnawing in his gut had only gotten worse after his brother called and cussed him out. But Christian was right. He was an ass, and he owed her an apology.

"What do you want?" Her voice came from behind the door. Obviously, at nearly eleven o'clock at night, she wasn't stupid enough to not look through the peephole and just open the door.

"I wanted to talk to you."

"You could have done that all night."

Ed ran his fingers through his hair. "Darcy, just let me in please."

She didn't say anything, and for a few moments he just stood there wondering if she'd walked away from the door, but then he heard the chain being removed and the deadbolt unlocking.

Slowly, the door opened and there stood Darcy McCary, looking more beautiful than he'd ever seen her and as pissed as any woman he'd ever seen, too.

Her makeup was still fresh, but she'd ridded herself of the rest of the night. This was how he liked to see women—relaxed. Dressed up and done up was fun, but this was when they let themselves be seen.

Ed stepped into the small, basement apartment, and Darcy slammed the door behind him. As if she were either comfortable with having him there—or didn't care, which was more likely— she walked to the corner of the room, picked up the remote to the TV, and then sat on couch and turned down the volume.

He stood for a moment and took in the sight of her watching Lucille Ball. She wasn't going to make this easy on him, and he knew he didn't deserve it.

"Listen, I just wanted to say I am sorry."

Darcy nodded, her eyes still on the TV. "Keep going."

That burned him. "I should have been there. That event was important for my aunt. I know my entire family was there, but I should have been there, too."

"You were covered, right? I mean, you sent your assistant. That should count."

"No. No." He walked around the side of the couch and stood in front of her. "That's not why I sent you—or invited you." He jammed his hands into his pockets and leaned back on his heels. "I wanted to be with you and introduce you to everyone."

"Christian did that."

He gritted his teeth. He'd never fought his brother over a woman. This might be the first.

"Darcy, I chickened out. And I'm sorry."

She shifted her eyes up to him, her lips pursed. "Chickened out? I've now met your entire family. Not one of them fearful in any way. So what would you have to chicken out about?"

"Being with you."

She let out a grunt and stood. "I'm not much to fear, Eduardo Keller."

She started to walk past him and he reached for her arm, pulling her back to him. Her breath gasped as she slammed into his chest. He didn't want to scare her, and he knew he hadn't when he saw the surprise in her eyes and heard the sigh.

"This has nothing to do with my family and everything to do with thinking that falling for my assistant might be the wrong thing to do."

Darcy's mouth opened as if she'd considered arguing, but she said nothing, which was worse.

Ed raised his hand to her cheek and caressed it with his thumb. She didn't back away.

"I was trying to talk myself out of this," he said softly as he slid his other hand down her arm until their fingers intertwined. "I have feelings for you and…"

His sentence was cut short when Darcy stood on the tips of her toes and placed a kiss against his lips.

Just as quickly, she backed up, turned for the kitchen, and disappeared.

Ed stood alone in the living room. He hadn't expected that. A slap across the face maybe, but not a kiss. Now what?

Slowly, he made his way to the kitchen. Darcy was standing over the sink, and her shoulders bounced as if she were crying.

"Are you all right?" He stepped up behind her.

"No, you idiot."

That was better. That was how he felt, too.

"Darcy, I didn't mean to…"

She turned, mascara ran down her cheeks, and her nose and lips were red and swollen from the cry she was having. She was absolutely adorable.

"Didn't mean to what? Tell me that you had feelings for me? Because I have feelings for you, too. But how stupid is all of this now?" She wiped her tears, which streaked black down her cheeks. "I can't work for you if we both have feelings. And I can't stay in Nashville if I don't have a job. And this is all so confusing and…" She shook her head as if she didn't want to continue.

Ed moved in closer and took her hands in his. "I didn't go tonight because I needed to separate myself from this. I thought that not going out with you socially would fix this thumping you cause in my chest."

Darcy sucked in a ragged breath, but her eyes had gone soft behind the tears that were drying.

He smiled. "It didn't work. Christian called and chewed me out. My mother did the same, but in her I'm disappointed voice, not her angry one, which is worse."

Darcy laughed.

Ed interlaced their fingers. "The consensus was they all loved you, but I knew they would. Such a mixed up lot—all brought together by chance and not birth. But they support each and every one of us. And I kind of think they support you over me now." This time he laughed, but Darcy's smile had subsided.

"What do you mean a family brought together by chance?"

She let him still hold her hands, and he found comfort in that. "I mean, the Kellers adopted three of their children. Most of us aren't blood related, but that isn't what makes a family."

"No, it's not." She looked away as if to gather her thoughts. "Who's adopted?"

"My dad."

"You're dad isn't a blood Keller?"

He grinned. "Didn't you notice he's a little dark?"

She shrugged. It hadn't really crossed her mind.

"He was adopted when he was seven. His parents had moved here from Puerto Rico, and the Kellers were friends of theirs through church. But my biological grandparents were killed in a car accident, and my father was the only survivor. My grandparents—the Kellers—took him in and became his parents."

"So you're not really a Keller?"

He lifted a brow, and Darcy shook her head.

"You know what I mean," she argued.

"I do."

"Who else?"

"Regan and Arianna. They're sisters, blood sisters, but they were adopted when Arianna was a toddler and Regan was an infant."

Darcy dropped her shoulders. How amazing was it that she'd never known anyone who'd been adopted before, and now here was this whole family who knew what she was going through. Was that what connected Regan and Zach? Then it hit her—if Zach and Mary Ellen were her parents, had Zach known? Didn't women who got in trouble give up babies all the time without the father knowing?

She felt the blood drain from her head, and Ed's hands moved from hers to her arms.

"Are you okay?"

"Yes." She swallowed hard. "I've never known anyone, ever, who was adopted."

Ed laughed. "And I only know those who have been."

She nodded. "I'm adopted."

Ed laughed again. "You don't say? Well, this must be fate, huh?"

It was a bold move, but he pulled her into his arms and she rested her head against his chest. This felt right. Maybe this could work.

CHAPTER 21

*D*arcy absorbed his embrace. She wasn't alone. Could this Keller family be the very thing she'd always needed and didn't know it? Maybe it was a waste to go after finding her parents. She had parents, and they were good ones. And, even if Zach was her father and Mary Ellen was her mother, did it matter? Would it be worth tearing apart this family just so she could have some peace of mind?

If nothing else, as she got closer to the Kellers, maybe she could have someone to talk to about all this silly adoption stuff. Wouldn't it be nice to have someone on her side who understood what she was thinking?

Suddenly, finding out who actually gave birth to her wasn't so important.

Darcy pulled back. "So now what? What are we going to do about all of this? I mean, can you at least help me find a new job?"

Ed focused his eyes on her. "Let me get this straight because it's been a long time since I've told a girl I like her." The corner of his mouth turned up, and the dimple in his cheek deepened. "So I like you, and you like me?"

Darcy dropped her shoulders and laughed. "Yes. I like you. An awful lot, I think."

Ed nodded and bit down on his lip. "So it would be safe to say that we're both willing to feel this thing out? You know," he said as he pulled her in closer, "I could call you my girlfriend?"

That made Darcy giggle. At this very moment in her life, she was glad he had a little bit of a childish side.

"Yes." She raised her arms around his neck. "I would very much like to be your girlfriend."

Ed rested his hands on her hips. "You're dad isn't going to come after me with a shot gun, is he? I'm a little older than you, and I've only known you a week."

"What did you say a little bit ago? This was fate?" Ed nodded, and Darcy rose on her toes again. "Then I think he'll be fine with it."

She pressed her lips to his, and his arms came around her in a possessive hold as if he were pulling her as close as two people could possibly get.

Ed deepened the kiss, and Darcy could feel every muscle in her body become fluid. Dear Lord, if this man could kiss like this —what else could he do?

When their lips parted, Darcy lowered herself back off her toes. "I'm a lucky girlfriend. You're a good kisser."

"You're not too bad yourself."

She swallowed hard and looked into his dark eyes. "Now what do we do?"

Ed lifted his hand to her cheek again and brushed it with his thumb. "I'm going to kiss you one more time and then I'm going to leave."

"Oh," the word choked out of her throat.

"I'm a gentleman above anything else. I stood you up, and I came to apologize."

"Yes, you did."

"So now I'm going to take my overheated body home and

jump into a cold shower. Then I'm going to meet you Monday morning at the office, and everything will be normal."

Darcy was feeling the pang of rejection shoot through her. "Okay, but I have to wait until Monday to see you again?"

Ed shrugged. "I have this meeting in Memphis tomorrow. It'll take most the day."

"That's right. I scheduled that."

"Yes, you did." He smiled. "Valerie will be glad to hear about us. She had way too many questions about you the other day."

Darcy wasn't sure how to take that, but she understood they were friends, and from what she'd learned about Valerie, she had no cause for worry.

Ed kissed her cheek. "I think I remember your coffee of choice. It'll be on your desk." He gave her nose a tweak with his finger.

She was feeling like a child herself now, and she wasn't sure what had transpired.

Ed leaned in and kissed her softly again, just as he said he was going to do. "And about that job. You have a perfectly good job with me. In one week, you've done more than a hundred temps have ever done. And Mary Ellen is very fond of you. That means a lot in the company."

Darcy hoped he didn't see her jaw clench.

He turned for the door. "There isn't any reason we can't work together."

"But your uncle fired your aunt."

"Circumstances were much different."

"How so?"

Ed only smiled. "They have their secrets." He nipped her forehead with a kiss. "By the way, I don't intend on keeping us a secret. I'm heading upstairs to tell my brother to stay dressed when you're around and to keep his hands off of you."

"He's never had his hands on me," she growled out.

"That's very reassuring."

Darcy was having second thoughts about this. He made her sound like a paid girlfriend—a kept woman perhaps. That wasn't what she was thinking when she'd said, so childishly, that she'd be his girlfriend.

"Goodnight." Ed turned and raced up the stairs.

Darcy shut and locked the door. She walked back to the couch and dropped down onto it.

Ed Keller was an interesting man, to say the least.

She buried her face in her hands. What was she doing? She liked him. She really did. And she was going to need a cold shower too, but getting involved with Ed was going to cost her everything. He held her job in his hands. Her house was under his control, too. Even her neighbor was part of this intertwined life. Now if something went wrong she'd lose her man, her job, her house, and a family she was falling in love with as much as she was with Ed.

What if she had stumbled upon the truth of her birth parents? Would that eventually mean the end of everything? And what kind of secrets did Zach and Regan have that caused him to fire her? Had Regan found out about him and Mary Ellen?

CHAPTER 22

*T*here was a different zip in Ed's step when he walked into the office with a bouquet of flowers and Darcy's coffee in his hand. It had been freeing to tell her how he felt and to kiss her on Saturday night.

Things were going to work out. He'd be damned if they didn't.

But, because he was a man who liked to thoroughly think things out and this thing with Darcy was the most spontaneous thing he'd ever done, he decided that if they didn't work out he'd relocate her in the company and they'd keep her rental agreement intact. That would ensure that she wouldn't have to run home to Kentucky just because he was an ass—because there was a great chance that just might prove to be his downfall.

He sat at his desk and started sifting through the bid sheets. By nine, he still hadn't heard what had become the familiar sound of her desk drawer opening. Maybe the bus was late.

Ed walked to the door and looked down the hall toward his uncle's office. Perhaps she'd stopped by Mary Ellen's desk. It wouldn't be odd for him to just walk down that way, poke his head in, and say hello.

Mary Ellen was attending to a phone call and gave him a nod to go into his uncle's office.

DARCY WALKED THROUGH THE DOORS OF THE HUMAN RESOURCE office with her new friend, Candy. Fate was working in some very strange ways when it came to her mission to find her birth parents.

Sure, Saturday night she'd warded it off, but today when she'd met Candy, things had changed.

She'd seen her on the bus all week, but one, thirty-minute conversation with the young woman, who had just been promoted in the department, and Darcy knew that maybe by the end of the day she could have all the answers to all of her questions.

However, she also knew that a job and her relationship with Ed hung in the balance. And if Candy got in trouble, Darcy would have to find a new route to work—if she kept her job.

Candy walked into her office and Darcy followed, shutting the door.

Candy turned on her computer. "This is kinda fun. Like being a private investigator."

Darcy nodded. Candy had never met Zach or Ed personally. She was just one of the hundreds of people that made the big corporation work. There was no fear, yet, that she'd cross paths with Ed.

She had, for some reason, told Candy everything about coming to Tennessee. Though she hadn't shared her story about Ed. As far as Candy knew, Darcy was a secretary two floors up.

"So you said you're twenty-four?" Candy asked.

"Yes."

"So you were born…" She did the calculation in her head and then hit a few keys on the computer.

Darcy sat down in the chair next to Candy's desk and waited for something—anything.

"Okay, what month?"

"August."

Candy nodded and wrinkled up her face. "So we're assuming the woman would have left in August, right? Perhaps on maternity leave or just quit."

Darcy shrugged as Candy scrolled through the list.

"I have seventeen people who left on maternity leave that year, but none in August."

That didn't seem right. Mary Ellen, Regan had said, had gone into labor the day she'd started.

"Look for Regan Keller and see what day she started working that year."

The name hadn't meant anything to Candy, obviously. She typed it in.

"Regan Keller was hired..." she searched, "in the spring and it says her job was terminated in August, but not until the year after you were born."

"After?" That couldn't be right. She swallowed hard. "Mary Ellen Rothchild. When did she go on maternity leave?"

Again, Candy typed in the name. "It says her last day before maternity leave was the same as Regan Keller's start date in the spring, but the year after you were born." Candy turned to her. "Are you sure they led you to the right place?"

Darcy wondered. She was sure the dates would add up, and she'd have something to take to Mary Ellen and Zach, if the opportunity offered itself.

"Well, I guess we hit a dead end," Candy said and closed the file. "But if you get more information, I'd love to help you. And I promise I won't tell a soul. I mean, I could lose my job for telling you what I did."

"I really appreciate it." Darcy stood to leave.

"Hey maybe we could go out some time. You know, double date. You said your boyfriend is native to Nashville. Maybe he could show us around."

Darcy didn't see that happening. Candy might not have met Ed, but she was sure she'd recognize him.

Darcy nodded. "Yeah, I'll see when he's free."

She gave her a wave and headed toward the elevator.

As the door closed and she watched the lit numbers in the elevator climb, she looked at her watch. It was already twenty after nine. Certainly Ed was going to notice she wasn't there. Their little relationship wasn't starting off on the best foot.

When the door opened, Darcy hurried down the hallway toward her desk, but stopped when Mary Ellen waved her over.

"Your boss was looking for you," she said with a grin.

"Oh. Yeah, I'm a little late. I stopped by HR to drop something off."

Mary Ellen waved it off. "I don't think he was worried. I think he just missed you."

Darcy nodded nervously. "I should get to my desk."

"Ed is in Zach's office. They said to have you come in when you get here."

Her mouth went dry. "They didn't say why, did they?"

Mary Ellen laughed. "You're jumpy this morning. Is everything all right?"

"Yes. I'm fine." Darcy looked at the closed office door. "Should I just go in?"

"I'll announce you." She stood from behind her desk and went to the door that separated the small outer office with Zach's. She tapped lightly and then pushed open the door. "Darcy is here."

She heard Zach say, "Send her in."

Mary Ellen stepped back with her grin straining to turn upward into an enormous smile. "Go on in."

Darcy adjusted her purse on her shoulder and headed into the office. Zach and Ed were there, seated at the desk, but on the couch, Regan and Simone sat drinking coffee.

"I thought maybe I'd scared you off." Ed stood and crossed to her as Mary Ellen shut the door. He took her hands in his and gave her a kiss on the cheek.

Darcy felt the surge of nerves rattle in her breathing as she realized everyone in the room was watching them. She hadn't even been this uncomfortable when she'd gone to the fundraiser and met Ed's family—alone.

Ed stepped back and looked her over. "Everything okay? Was your bus late?"

Darcy shook her head. "No. I just had to drop some things off at HR." It wasn't a right out lie. She'd walked Candy to her desk and lingered, that's all.

"Oh, good." He turned toward Regan and Simone, who both sat on the couch hiding their grins behind gourmet coffee cups. "Simone and Regan want to take you to brunch and shopping."

Darcy bit down on her lip. "Oh, thank you, but I have so much to do. And I was late. Really, thank you, but I'm just getting settled. I can't really go shopping."

Simone stood first and crossed to them. "Brunch then. It is a perk to being one of the Benson/Keller women."

Darcy looked at Ed, who nodded. She now wished he'd kept them a secret a bit longer.

Regan crossed over to them. "I wasn't very comfortable when she did this to me either." She laughed. "Zach threw me into the limo with Simone and sent me to his mother."

"I didn't throw you in a limo," he scoffed from across the room.

"If I'm not mistaken though, you did make me go to lunch at your mother's, and you didn't show up."

Darcy saw Ed's jaw clench and then turned back as she heard Regan laugh.

"He set me up," she whispered. Regan turned back to the

couch and picked up her purse. "Ed, we'll have her back in a few hours."

"Take care of her," he said as he reached for Darcy's hand at her side and gave it a squeeze.

"As if she were my own daughter," Regan said, holding her hand up in a pledge.

CHAPTER 23

*T*hey had a car waiting out front and Darcy, though comfortable with the women, felt as though her nerves were going to have her sticking her head out the window and throwing up. How could she be so nervous?

Simone examined her manicure as they pulled away from the building. She spoke as eloquent as a princess, Darcy thought. What could possibly make a woman give up the oil-heiress life to move to America and live in the South?

Regan, though very put together in her own right, had a more laid-back style. Her dark hair had a few steaks of silver, but she didn't seem worried by it. And her clothes, though very nice, were obviously off the rack, where as Simone might have had her white suit pants custom made, they fit so well.

"So how do you like your job?" Regan asked, setting a gentle hand on Darcy's clenched ones.

"So far it has been very nice."

"Ed is a super kid." She laughed. "Oh, he's in his thirties, and I still think he's a kid."

Simone crossed her legs and bounced her foot. "He is very much in love with you."

Darcy felt the blood drain from her cheeks. "Oh, I don't think it's love. We certainly have an attraction and a comfort, but..."

"You do not believe in love at first sight?"

Had Ed put them up to this? "No. Well, I don't think I do."

"I do." Simone looked out the window. "My Curtis was mine from the moment I laid eyes on him."

"As soon as she left my husband alone," Regan retorted and both women laughed.

Simone shifted a glance to Darcy. "Regan, we scared her."

Regan's soft eyes soothed her. There was great comfort in this woman. "Simone grew up with Zach."

"Oh."

"We went to boarding school with each other in France. I loved him with my whole heart, that silly American boy. And he loved me like a sister." Simone let out a grunt and that made Darcy finally smile.

"You might imagine I was a bit threatened by her," Regan added.

"And you were foolish," Simone replied.

Regan shrugged and then turned her attention back to Darcy. "Do you have any brothers or sisters?"

"No. I'm an only child. My parents are much older, and I lost my mother last year to cancer."

Simone's hand went to her chest, and her eyes grew sad. Regan, again, touched Darcy's hands, and a tranquil feeling filled her.

"I'm sorry to hear that."

"Thank you."

Regan sat back. "So your father, he's still back in Kentucky? Isn't that where you're from?"

"Yes, ma'am. I needed to," she chose her words carefully, "find myself."

Regan's eyes darkened, and the corners of her mouth turned down. "I understand that. I tried to find myself once, too."

This time, Simone rested her hand on Regan's, and they both gave each other an understanding look, which meant something to both of them.

But only a moment later, Simone's smile returned. "Tell me, Darcy, why did you choose to come here and work?"

There was little she could tell these two women, even though she was now having doubts about Mary Ellen and Zach being her birth parents. That, she figured, had just been quick, wishful thinking. She'd fallen into everything else so easily.

"I was born in Nashville. I suppose I felt as though I had some connection."

Regan's eyes seemed to catch hers. "You were born in Nashville, and then your family moved to Kentucky?"

"My father was a military doctor. We did a lot of moving around the first few years of my life."

Regan's face softened. "That sounds nice."

Simone waved her hands. "Do you know if you were born at Nashville General?"

"Yes. I know that I was." Had she said too much?

"My husband was in emergency medicine for years there. Funny that you might have been born while he was there."

Darcy swallowed hard. Interesting. She wondered how she could get a lunch date with Curtis Keller.

DARCY'S BRUNCH WITH SIMONE AND REGAN PROVED TO BE absolutely wonderful. Those two women could talk up a storm, giggle like little girls, and eerily read each other's thoughts.

Darcy walked back to her desk and realized it was nearly one o'clock. There would be no catching the express bus tonight. However, she was sure she could convince her boss to drive her home.

Her heart gave a little hitch when she thought of just how much she did want to take him home.

She tapped on Ed's door after she'd deposited her purse in her desk drawer. As she opened it, she could see him at his desk, his head in his hand and the phone pressed to his ear with his other hand.

His morning hadn't looked to be as pleasant as hers had.

When he noticed her, he waved her in as though he needed her urgently. Then he pointed to the chair as if she was a child and he needed her to sit.

She did so. There was no need to think things were going to be nice and sweet at the office.

Darcy hadn't quite picked up on what was happening, but there was something wrong with a build. She also noticed that the phone was on an internal line. Could the voice on the other end of that call, which she could almost hear perfectly, be Zach?

"I got it. I got it." Ed shook his head. "I can get there by eight if I can catch a flight." He nodded. "No. This is my responsibility, and I'll take care of it. I'm not fifteen anymore. I don't need to take you or John with me."

Again, he listened for a moment, and then his face softened and he laughed. "I'm sure Valerie would love to go with me. This is right up her alley."

He hung up the phone, and his face grew hard again. "How was brunch?"

"Very nice."

He nodded curtly and gathered up the stack of papers on his desk. "I need you to book me a flight for Saint Louis for tonight. I'll need my own car, so arrange that as well. Then get on the phone and call Carson Maguire. He'll need to meet me on site." He waved his hands around as though to clear the slate. "Actually, get Valerie on the phone for me. She's going to have to go with me."

Darcy sat there and absorbed everything he'd just thrown at her.

He narrowed his eyes. "You can do this, right?"

"Yes, sir." She pushed herself up from her seat. "I'll see that it is all done within the hour."

She turned to leave, but Ed had moved from behind his desk and in front of her before she could even clear the chair.

"You can handle me at work, right? I mean, nothing here changes even if we are going to see each other."

"I didn't expect special treatment. The 'aunt ambush' threw me off this morning. But I understand what my responsibilities are."

"Ambush. Do you think I set that up?"

"Well, you have a lot to lose if you decided you had feelings for some psycho that you ran into and gave her a job because you felt sorry for her."

"You think I felt sorry for you?"

"Why else did you run me up here and give me a job?"

His mouth dropped open. "Because I read your resume."

She really hadn't considered that he thought she was actually qualified for the job.

"Darcy, I didn't send my aunts to grill you for information. You're an honest and hardworking woman. There is no reason for me to try and learn about you through others."

Darcy bit down on her lip. She was going to need to come clean with him if she wanted to keep him.

"Ed…" she started when his phone rang again.

He let out a grunt. "This build is going to kill me. I have to get that. We're okay?"

She nodded. He hurried back to his desk and picked up the line to his uncle again, and Darcy went back to her desk.

She clasped her hands together and let out a long breath. When they'd had that one intimate moment in her apartment, she thought she could handle "Ed the boss," but that was going to take some work. And she was very willing to try. Her feelings had moved way past like—she was slipping into love and that scared her to death.

Within the hour, everything he'd asked her to accomplish had been done. He'd be gone for the next three days in Saint Louis. She would be alone.

Her mind began to work overtime.

She'd have three days to get to know Curtis Keller. Maybe he remembered a warm, August day twenty-four years ago.

CHAPTER 24

*B*y four o'clock, Darcy fully understood the issues they were having in Saint Louis. Valerie had run into Ed's office an hour earlier, as well as Zach and Mary Ellen. The firm of Benson, Benson, and Hart had just encountered their first weather catastrophe that had shut down production.

A string of storms had brought three tornados down on the outskirts of Saint Louis. The severe storm had compromised the integrity of the building's structure. The foreman had been trying to clear the site of workers when a beam, which hadn't been completely fastened, fell and narrowly missed him.

The meeting around Ed's desk was frantic. Everyone was trying to get everything in place.

It was almost six o'clock by the time everyone had gone their separate ways, and Ed hurried to get the last of his papers together for the flight.

"You're not going to have time to go home and pack anything," Darcy said as she handed him the documents for his flight.

"I'll get some clothes there, and I can buy a toothbrush at the hotel." He opened the folder she'd handed him. "Good, this is the hotel closest to the site, right?"

"Just across the street."

He nodded in a way that she knew she'd done a good job.

She looked at her watch one more time and realized that the last bus toward her house had left ten minutes ago. There was no way she was going to ask him for a ride home at this point, but she wasn't going to mention not having one either. When he left, she'd call Christian and see if he was available.

"I really should have had you book yourself on this flight," he said as he shoved files into his shoulder bag. "I could use you to keep things straight."

"I'll be here when you need me, and I can make sure everything on this end runs smoothly and that you're not bothered by petty things."

For the first time in hours, Ed looked up at her and the thin hint of a smile formed on his lips. He set down his case.

"Come here." He held his hand out to her.

Darcy moved around the desk and set her own notebook next to his bag.

Ed took her in his arms and pulled her close to him. She could hear his heart beating in his chest. He didn't want to have to deal with the trauma that awaited him. She could tell by the way he held her in his arms.

He smoothed his hand over her hair. "I'm going to miss you. It's crazy that in the past few days I've only had a few moments with you."

"It's not like you're going to be gone forever."

"Yeah, but I'd like to have gotten in a lot more kissing."

Darcy sighed against his chest as he chuckled.

Ed leaned back and placed his finger under her chin. "When I get back, I just want to wrap you in my arms for an entire weekend. We can turn off all our phones, lock the door, and never come out."

"I like that."

He leaned in and brushed her lips with his lightly, and then again, but this time he deepened the kiss.

Ed lowered his hands and wrapped his arms tightly around her waist as she lifted her arms around his neck.

This was a moment she'd bring back into her thoughts when the man who was her boss snuck through and ruined the image of the man she loved. This delicate, dreamy, mind-blowing kiss would be her go-to thought when she needed him and he wasn't there.

Ed rested his forehead against hers. "Do you think you're okay to drive in Nashville?"

Darcy's head was still swimming, but she opened her eyes and looked up at him. "I suppose so. Why?"

"Drive me to the airport. Kiss me again like that before I leave."

That was it. There was no more indecision on whether she loved this man or not. Darcy McCary was head over heels in love with Eduardo Keller.

DARCY PULLED UP IN FRONT OF THE HOUSE AT NEARLY TEN o'clock. Letting go of Ed had been one of the hardest things she'd ever done. There was a truth that he'd have to travel with his job —a lot. She was going to need to get used to him not being with her.

As she turned off the engine to Ed's truck, she noticed that the house was fully illuminated. Three more cars were parked in front, and she could see people moving about.

She let out a sigh. She was tired. Hopefully Christian wasn't having a party.

She climbed out of the truck and was headed toward the house when the front door opened and Simone stepped out.

"Darcy, I'm glad it's you. I thought maybe Ed had missed his flight."

"No. I took him to the airport. Is everything all right?"

Simone folded her arms and walked down the front steps. "The downfall of being married to a doctor." She nodded to the house. "Christian tore a muscle at practice, and Curtis came by to check it out."

"Don't they have team doctors for that?"

Simone laughed. "Yes, but Curtis is very protective of his nephews and his niece. You'd think they were all his children, even if they are grown adults."

Darcy couldn't imagine such a network of people rallying around one person. Even when her mother was dying, it was only her and her father there to take care of her.

Simone touched her arm. "You should come in and say hello." It, however, wasn't just a suggestion. Simone took her arm and led her into the house.

Christian leaned back in the recliner while Curtis sat on a chair next to him, wrapping up his leg.

"Hey, look who came to my party," he said, obviously having had something to numb his pain.

"Are you okay?"

"Happens all the time." He smiled, and his eyes glossed over.

A moment later, Christian's mother came from the kitchen with a glass of water and a sandwich on a plate.

"Hello, Darcy."

Darcy felt her palms began to sweat at the thought of Ed's mother talking to her. The other night it had been fine—but now things were different.

"Hello, Mrs. Keller."

"Oh, you can call me Madeline." She smiled and turned to Christian. "Here, eat this before those pain meds make you sick."

The front door opened, and Carlos Keller walked in. "Curtis, just cut it off. He doesn't need it as a catcher."

"Funny, Dad."

Carlos gave a nod in Darcy's direction. "Hey, Darcy."

"Hello, Mr. Keller."

He walked over next to her and put his arm around her shoulders. "It's Carlos."

She only smiled as he walked toward his wife and gave her a kiss on the cheek.

"Okay, I think that'll do it." Curtis stood from his seat and stretched his back. "You know, if you do that too many times you're going to need surgery."

"Great. Nothing like not making it to the show and hurting this bad."

"Crybaby." Curtis laughed and headed to the kitchen.

Darcy smiled. This was probably a very serious situation to Christian, but the family dynamic was amazing to her. She couldn't get over the serious and the silly banter being mixed together and each person participating. Her parents were always very serious people. Everything was always so planned and thought out. This family came together, all in separate cars, at ten o'clock at night, and it seemed that no matter what, there could be humor and love.

"Did Ed get out okay?" Madeline asked.

"Yes. I just dropped him off at the airport."

Carlos looked out the window. "You drove his truck?"

"Yes," her voice creaked out.

Carlos and Madeline exchanged glances, and then Carlos smiled. "He doesn't let anyone touch that truck."

Darcy swallowed hard. That was a serious sign of commitment. Southern men took their trucks very seriously. Even her father never let her drive his truck.

She forced a smile to her lips and then directed her attention to Christian. "I'm going to unlock the doors between my place and yours and leave it open. If you need anything, just yell and I can come up and help you."

He gave her a groggy grin then looked up at his mother. "He told me I had to keep my hands off her."

Madeline shook her head, and Darcy could feel the heat rise up in her cheeks.

"Christian, fall asleep before you stick that foot down your throat." Madeline kissed him on the forehead and headed into the kitchen.

Carlos turned off the lamp and grabbed the quilt off the back of the couch. He gently laid it over Christian, who was already battling droopy eyelids.

Darcy didn't know what they'd given him, but it seemed to be working.

Carlos followed everyone to the kitchen. Darcy walked past Christian, and he reached for her. Even half asleep he seemed to be quick with the only woman in a room.

"Thanks for offering to take care of me."

"You're welcome."

His eyes closed. "He's a very lucky man," he said just as he dozed off.

CHAPTER 25

*a*s Darcy looked down at the man who resembled the man she loved, she realized all of this could be hers. Not the house or the cherished truck, but this family dynamic. She could have it all.

When she walked into the kitchen, the talking stopped. There was tension in the air, but then again, she assumed that it was only her.

"I was just going to unlock the door," she said, pointing to the staircase.

"I got it," Curtis said as he ran down the steps and clicked the inside lock. "This one is ready."

Darcy looked around the room as Curtis ran back up the stairs.

"Well then, I guess I'll head down."

She started toward the back door when Madeline stopped her. "Christian might wake up in about an hour in some pain. The medicine is in the cupboard behind the peanut butter." She pointed to the corner.

"Okay."

"It's a mother thing. If I hide it then he can't get to it if he's feeling loopy."

Very clever, she thought.

"If I hear him, I'll come up."

"Thanks for taking care of him—and Ed. I know that this trip isn't going to be an easy one on him, but he said he was glad he had you to take care of everything."

"That's my job." She gave everyone a wave and headed out the back door.

"I'll walk you down," Curtis said and followed her.

Darcy walked down the steps of the patio to the stairwell which led to her apartment with Curtis right behind her.

As Darcy pushed open her door, she turned to Curtis. "Thanks for seeing me home."

He reached into his pocket and pulled out a card. "If he needs anything, just give me a call." He handed her the card. "This is the second time he's hurt himself like this." He shook his head. "Reason I never played too many sports."

Darcy looked down at the card and then back up at him. She swallowed hard. "Your wife said you used to work in emergency medicine at Nashville General."

"I sure did. I've only been at the clinic full time for the past five years."

Darcy nodded. "I was born at that hospital."

"No kidding? But you're from Kentucky?"

"Yes."

Curtis smiled. "Well, you never know. If your mom came through emergency, maybe I saw her...or you." He gave her a wink and a wave and headed back up the stairs.

Darcy looked down at the card in her hand. Every time she thought she could forget about finding her birth parents, another opportunity arrived. And, once again, it was from within the Keller family that she could maneuver another piece of information.

This was the second time in a day that Curtis Keller had been considered for her source of information. If the Kellers were as tight as she'd witnessed, Curtis would be back tomorrow to check in on Christian.

It was time to come up with a clever reason to start a conversation with him. Perhaps he knew someone who could access files, just as Candy had in the HR department. If she could only get to someone who could type her birthdate into the database at the hospital, surely there'd be a hit.

It was two o'clock in the morning when she was startled awake by someone calling her name. It took her a moment to realize it was Christian.

She stumbled out of bed, nearly falling into the wall when her legs tangled in the bedding. Darcy kicked it away and hurried up the stairs and through the dark kitchen.

"Are you okay?" she croaked out.

"I have to pee," he retorted in a groggy voice.

She knew it was a serious thing, but at the same time, there was a part of her who wanted to smack him on the back of the head for waking her up.

"How exactly am I supposed to help you do that?"

"By getting me the crutches my dad moved over against the wall."

"Oh." Even in the dark of the hour, she could feel her cheeks heat.

She walked across the room and retrieved the crutches. She clicked on the lamp, and they both winced at the light as their eyes adjusted.

Christian wiggled toward the end of the chair, and Darcy did what she could to help him up. Once he was balanced, she took a step back.

He grinned. "You're cute in your pajamas."

As he slowly headed to the bathroom, Darcy looked down to realize she'd worn some very short shorts to bed and the tank top she had on was more than a little revealing. It was obviously colder down in the basement.

While Christian was occupied, she ran down to her place, pulled on a sweatshirt, and ran back up the stairs as he was coming out of the bathroom.

He gave her a sideways glance and smiled. "You didn't have to change for me."

She let out a grunt. "How's your leg?"

"Throbbing. Achy. Stupid."

This time, he made his way to the couch and very skillfully let himself down on the cushion. Obviously it wasn't the first time he'd dealt with crutches. She was sure that if he hadn't been on pain meds, he would have tried to have gotten them himself without her assistance.

"Can I get you anything?"

Christian pulled his leg up onto the couch and adjusted it to rest on a pillow. "I could really use another pain pill and a piece of toast."

Darcy nodded and turned toward the kitchen.

"By the way," Christian called out, and she turned back to him. "The pills are behind the peanut butter."

Darcy smiled. "How do you know that?"

He laughed. "I know her too well. She's my mom, after all."

CHAPTER 26

*D*arcy chuckled to herself as walked into the kitchen to make Christian some toast. As she reached into the cupboard for the pills, a pang of regret filled her chest. She missed her mother.

She'd been so angry about finding out she was adopted and then about her mother getting sick—she'd forgotten to appreciate her for a long time.

The first tear broke loose.

If her mother were still alive to take care of her had she been hurt, she'd have sat in that chair next to her the entire night. There'd have been a little light on in the corner and a never-empty glass of water next to her on a table.

The flood gate opened and she sobbed.

Had she been a good enough daughter that when her mother died she felt as though she'd done a good job? She hadn't been a troublesome kid. Darcy was a good student and well-liked, but was she as kind to her parents as the Kellers were to theirs?

And now, how did she honor her? She was in Tennessee digging around as if her mother had taken away her life by not telling her she was adopted. Perhaps there was a reason behind that.

Darcy covered her mouth and tried to stifle the sobs, but it was no use.

"Darcy, are you okay?"

She'd never been a quiet crier. She sucked in a breath. "Yes. I'll be out in a sec."

Darcy hurried and made him a slice of toast, filled a glass with water, and poured out a pain pill—making sure to put the bottle back behind the peanut butter.

When she walked back into the room, Christian was sitting up on the couch, but in the shadows of the lamp, he looked so much like Ed her heart ached a little more.

"Were you crying?" Christian asked as she handed him the piece of toast and his pill.

"I was having a moment. I'm sorry."

She handed him the glass of water, and he swallowed his pill and looked up at her as she took the glass and set it on the table.

"Why are you sorry? What's wrong?"

Darcy tried to shake it away, but there were still more tears to fall.

"Oh, come here." Christian pulled her down beside him and wrapped his arm around her shoulders. "What's going on?"

"I'm just missing my mama." She wiped at her cheeks. "You said you knew your mom well enough to know where she hid the pills, and it made me miss my mom."

Christian smoothed his hand over her hair. "Your mom—is she…"

"She died of cancer last year."

"Oh." He let out a long sigh. "I'm so sorry. My mom had cancer."

"Ed told me."

"Did she suffer long?"

Darcy shook her head. "She went within a year. And if she

was suffering, you'd never have known. She occupied herself with my well-being."

Christian chuckled. "She sounds like my mom. She went through a double mastectomy without telling a soul."

Darcy turned and looked at him. "She was alone?"

He shrugged. "You've met this family. Do you think they'd let her get away with that?"

Darcy shook her head.

"She and my dad were divorced back then, and my step-dad had left her. We didn't know that then. But she thought she could go through that alone, and no one would worry about her."

"She needed people. That's a major surgery."

"Uncle Curtis saw her being wheeled into surgery and called my dad. He was by her side every moment."

"Was she grateful? Or was she mad?"

"Both, but in the end it bonded our family back together. They're happier now than they ever were."

Christian pulled her closer to him.

"It's okay to miss her."

"I know. I just hope I was the daughter she'd always wanted."

"I can't imagine you let her down."

Darcy let out a sigh. "I was angry when she got sick, but not just because she was sick." She bit down on her lip. It was okay to talk about it, she decided. "The year before they had told me I was adopted."

"You're adopted?"

"Yes, and I felt like my whole life was a sham. That was something I should have known from the start."

"Would it have made a difference?"

She shrugged. "I don't know. But I was so upset that I was angry with her while she was dying. Then I left and came here to find my roots." Now she'd said too much.

"You came to Tennessee to find your birth parents?"

He was quick, and she wasn't sure she wanted that at two-thirty in the morning. "It was a thought."

"I'm laid up. Maybe I can help."

She patted his chest and sat up. "Thanks. I'm rethinking it now. I should honor the parents I had, not try to find new ones. Besides, if I'm honest with myself, they gave me away because they didn't want a baby. So why would they want an adult?"

Saying that aloud nearly made it impossible to think she'd even wanted to find them. But had she not made her journey, she'd never have met Ed Keller. She missed him terribly at the moment.

Darcy scooted off the couch and looked down at Christian, whose eyes were growing heavy.

"I'm going back to bed. Yell again if you need me."

"I will."

She turned to walk away.

"Darcy," he called after her, and she turned back to him. "Some of the very best people I know are adopted, and they don't know their birth parents. It doesn't make them any less important to this family."

She smiled and nodded. If she'd been looking for a family to belong to, she'd found it. There was no need to cause herself any more restless nights.

The clock on the microwave read two-fifty-six. First thing when she woke up she was going to call her father and tell him that she loved him. It was time to honor the parents that gave her a life—and forget about the ones who gave her life.

CHAPTER 27

*D*arcy had tried to reach her father on her way into work, but he'd never answered. He'd call back when he had a moment. He always did.

Now she sat at her desk and answered emails that were coming in and went about with business as usual. The only difference was the door to Ed's office was open, but he wasn't there.

When the phone rang, she answered it as she would any other phone call that came into his office, but this time when she heard the voice on the other end, her heart did a little flip in her chest.

"Good morning, sweetheart."

She sighed. "Good morning. How is Saint Louis?"

"It'll be better around dinner time."

"Why is that?" There was a flirty tone to her voice.

"Because you're going to book yourself a flight out here and spend the week with me."

Now the flip in her heart became a weight in her stomach. "I am?"

"There are multiple reasons. I need you to help me coordinate these meetings with insurance companies and city officials. I can only do so much of this without losing my mind."

She'd thought maybe he'd wanted her there because he was missing her, but this was her boss calling. There was a serious difference.

"No problem. I'll make arrangements, and I'll meet you at the site." Her voice threatened to give out on her, but she could be a professional and keep it together.

"Shall I go by your house and pick you up a suitcase of clothes?"

He laughed. "No. I took care of all that. You might leave me a small corner of yours to carry it all back in though."

She didn't say anything.

"Darcy, above all else, I want you here because I miss you. Us being apart is no way to start a relationship."

She dropped her shoulders, releasing the tension that had built up in them.

"You really miss me?"

"I know it probably sounds crazy since we've only known each other a week, but it's true."

She figured she was smiling like a fool, but she had needed to hear it. "My mother always told me it wouldn't matter how long I knew a man, when you knew he was the right one you knew."

Ed chuckled. "My grandmother would say the same thing."

"I'm still old fashioned enough though. I'm going to book myself a room."

"I wouldn't have it any other way."

She knew he meant that too, or he would have stayed the other night—or asked to.

Darcy made the arrangements Ed had asked her to make. She then headed home to pack up her suitcase.

She parked out back by the garage where Christian's car was parked. As she climbed down out of Ed's truck, she wondered if she should stay home. Maybe Christian would need help.

Then she laughed at the thought. She'd never known a family that swarmed around anyone who needed help as much as the Kellers did. He'd be fine.

But, before she headed down to pack up, she'd check in on him.

As usual, the back door was unlocked. She tapped on it as she opened it.

"Christian, can I come in?" she called out.

"Yeah, come on in. We're in the front room."

We're? She hadn't seen another car. But, sure enough, when she walked into the front room, there was Tyler sitting with Christian playing Xbox.

"You look like you're feeling better," she said.

"Yeah, just bored. Tyler had the day off so we're playing baseball—sorta."

Tyler was focused on the game, and when he'd scored a home run, he jumped from his chair with a holler.

Darcy laughed. She'd seen boys play games like this, but these were grown men.

"Sorry, Darcy, I was concentrating. How are you?" Tyler asked.

"I'm good. I'm heading to Saint Louis."

Christian looked up at her. "You're going out there to be with Ed?"

She bit down on her lip. "Yes."

"I'll say it again. He's a lucky man."

"But what about you? I feel bad leaving you here."

Christian shrugged. "Why? I'm well taken care of."

Tyler jumped up again. "And I thought you were some kind of baseball player. Look at that score."

"You'd better go," Christian said. "I have to school this boy."

They all laughed and Darcy turned to walk away, but something made her turn back when Tyler began to talk smack to Christian. There was something very familiar about him. He was blond and fair like his father, but that wasn't the familiar part. She couldn't quite touch on it, but there was something.

DARCY STARED AT HER SUITCASE AND MENTALLY COUNTED THE items. It was a business trip after all, not a vacation. Trying to decide if a swimsuit was necessary was a waste of time.

She closed the case and hauled it out of her room. Food at the airport was horribly expensive, so she decided to make herself a sandwich. At the moment, her living expenses weren't very high, but the need to save money was going to be very important. She was rather enjoying driving Ed's truck, and it wouldn't be long before she'd want a car of her own.

An hour later, she was in the truck and headed to the airport. She'd just merged onto the highway, which had her jumpy, when her cell phone rang.

Darcy growled. She reached next to her, and with one hand, she dug through her purse until she found her phone.

"Hello."

"Hey, honey, it's Daddy."

Darcy sighed. "Hi, Daddy. How are you?"

"I'm good. I got your message this morning. I went to breakfast with Pete and Greg."

"Coffee crew, huh?"

"They keep me sane."

She didn't like that, but she knew it was true.

"So, what were you calling for?"

Darcy focused on the road ahead of her, trying not to let her emotions take over.

"I was just missing you and thinking about mom."

"Everything is okay? Your job is good?"

"Everything is wonderful, Daddy. I'm actually on my way to Saint Louis right now to meet my boss." Why did she say it that way?

"You be careful. I'm not fond of you being away from me, but now you're traveling…"

And that was why she'd said it that way. "Daddy, I'm fine."

"Your boss is a nice man?"

Darcy smiled. "He's the best."

Her father growled. "You're not ready to come home yet, are you? I still don't see why you had to go to Nashville to work. You know, Pete's son…"

"Daddy, I'm fine. I don't need a job from Pete's son or anyone else. I landed a great job, and I'm very happy."

"I worry about you. You know your mother would have been sick over you moving."

Darcy's hand was tightening on the steering wheel. If they'd only told her the truth to start with, she wouldn't be worrying her father.

"It's time for me to spread my wings."

"You're always welcome to come home."

Darcy took her exit and started toward the airport. "I know. Daddy, I have to go. But remember, I love you very much."

"Take care of yourself."

Darcy hit the button on her cell phone and tossed it back into her purse. Her father had a hard time expressing his true feelings. But even though he never ended his phone calls by saying he loved her, she knew he did. Darcy pulled into the parking garage and began to search for a spot that was big enough for Ed's truck.

CHAPTER 28

$\mathcal{E}$d rubbed his eyes and then leaned his head back against the couch in his hotel room. He'd forgotten to get Darcy's itinerary, and he hadn't been able to reach her on her cell phone. She was probably in flight.

He'd wanted to be at the airport when she arrived. He owed her that much.

It looked like their stay in Saint Louis might last at least three more days. He'd rather spend time with her without the interruption of getting this build back on track, but he had to remember she was his assistant.

He was walking a thin line between keeping it professional and losing his mind. There had been no choice but to have her fly out to meet him. Sure, she could have done everything he needed her to do from Nashville, but the truth was he couldn't focus.

There had never been a time when a woman had seemed so perfect in his life, and the crazy part was he didn't really know her at all.

His grandmother had always said that when the right woman came along he'd just know it, but he'd never believed it.

And what was it about her? Why this woman who ran into

him and then blamed him? But that hadn't been it. There had been more on her mind than just finding a job. Fate had put her in his path, but why?

He lifted his head and stood from the couch just as there was a knock on his door. It was probably Valerie. They'd discussed getting a bite, but he'd wanted to try and get a hold of Darcy first.

Ed pulled open the door and was more than pleasantly surprised to find Darcy standing on the other side. She was dressed in a simple, black dress with a shawl draped over her arm. Her makeup was fresh, and her smile slightly seductive.

"You owe me a dinner, and if they play music, you owe me a dance, too."

"You look beautiful."

"Thank you."

"How did you know where to find me?"

"Valerie, who by the way says she has plans for dinner already."

He laughed. "I'll bet she does." Ed reached for her hand and pulled her though the door.

As soon as she was in front of him, he shut the door, pressed her up against it, and his mouth came down on hers.

She moaned as his tongue found hers, and his heart rate kicked up. Any other woman—any other time—he might forget his gentlemanly promise and carry her to the bed only a few feet away. But this was different. This was Darcy, and there was time. Time to kiss. Time to caress. Time to wait.

Ed ran his finger down her throat and then followed with his mouth. He could feel her pulse beneath his lips. Her heart was racing as fast as his. Her breath was in his ear, and her fingers gripped tightly to the back of his shirt.

It wouldn't take much persuading. She'd give into his needs as a man, this much he knew. But he couldn't—wouldn't—do that.

Ed nuzzled his face into her neck and felt her body quake against his.

"Oh, I did miss you," he whispered in her ear.

She gasped for a breath. "I missed you, too."

"It's a good thing you got your own room. This is truly a test of my good behavior."

She chuckled in his ear and then pressed a kiss to his ear. "Ed, I'm not a virgin. You don't have to worry about that."

He pulled back and gazed into her dark eyes. "I'm not worried about hurting you. I'm more focused on keeping you."

"Oh," she said on a sigh.

"I have never felt this way about someone. I don't even really know you, but..."

"I know." She smiled. "I know."

Ed sucked in a breath. "Let's go to dinner. Suddenly my head is swimming."

"I could use a decent meal."

ED SAT IN THE BOOTH ACROSS FROM DARCY IN THE RESTAURANT IN the hotel. It wasn't a five-star establishment, but it wasn't some downtown dive either.

Darcy was glad she hadn't missed him by the time she got to the hotel, cleaned up, and met him in his room. Her phone had died during the flight. She was just glad it had all worked out.

Once their order was taken, Ed reached across the table for her hand. "How was your night last night?"

She chuckled. "Eventful. So you don't let people drive your truck?"

Ed's brows narrowed. "Who told you that?"

"Your dad."

"You were with my dad last night?"

Darcy smiled. "And your mother, brother, Aunt Simone, and Uncle Curtis too."

"I leave town and they invite you to spend time with them?"

She laughed then covered her mouth with her hand to stifle it. "No. Christian tore a muscle in his leg."

Ed's face tightened in concern, and he leaned in over the table. "He's okay? No one called me."

"Relax. He's fine. They knew you were busy." She took a sip from her water glass. "Curtis says if he does it again he might need surgery. But he was in good spirits when I left today. Tyler was keeping him company. They were playing baseball on Xbox."

That made Ed laugh, and he relaxed back into his seat. "That's the second time he's done that. The first one cost him his chance at major league."

"I think he's upset about it, but he seems to be taking it in stride."

Ed nodded. "You seem to have spent more time with my family in the past week than I have in weeks."

"That's not my fault."

Ed held his free hand up in defense. "I know. I'm sorry."

"I love your family, and it's given me some peace."

"My family gives you peace?"

"Yes." She grinned. "I was so mad when I found out I was adopted that I almost didn't even speak to my parents for a year. Then when my mother got sick, I was mad that she was sick. Don't get me wrong. I took care of her, but I was mad."

"I remember being mad. I was mad because it wasn't fair to me that my mom was sick."

Darcy dropped her shoulders. "Exactly." They did have a lot in common. "Anyway, I never had anything like you do. I had mom and dad, and that was it. You have this enormous family who cares for each other and takes in strays. I feel like I belong there."

Ed rubbed his thumb over her knuckles. "You do belong there."

.   .   .

THE SENTIMENT WAS TRUE AND FROM HIS HEART. ED WASN'T thinking marriage and the longevity of their relationship, but it was there, tucked in the back of his mind. He'd seen how his family took to her.

Sure, his family was kind to strangers, and they took care of each other. That was a fact. But there had been something about her that had drawn them all to her. A comfort none of them had ever had with anyone he brought home.

That was probably why Christian was drawn to her, too. She was comfortable to be around. She was familiar.

They enjoyed their dinner and then sat at the bar and had a drink. Or to be more specific, Ed had a drink and Darcy had water.

"I've seen you drink a beer. But not tonight?" he asked.

"I need to keep my head screwed on tight, as my father would say."

He thought maybe he'd need a few more to keep his from reeling about taking her upstairs.

Ed looked at his watch, and it was inching toward eleven o'clock. "I suppose we should finish our drinks and turn in. We have an insurance meeting in the morning at seven-thirty."

Darcy cleared her throat and set down her glass. "That's mighty early."

"Oh, that's just the first meeting." He smiled.

"Sounds like a delightful day."

The band was still playing, and the song had slowed. "What do you say we take this night out with a spin on the dance floor?"

"I think that sounds perfect."

Ed took her hand and led her to the small dance floor. The room was empty except for a few couples in booths sharing drinks and a few business men talking business. But as he took her in his arms, the rest of the world faded away.

He stood a head taller than she did, and she was small in his arms. But this woman wasn't fragile. She was strong, both in body and mind. Whatever it took, he was going to keep her in his grasp for the rest of his life.

Darcy draped her arms around his neck and pressed her body close to his.

"You haven't taken any of your other assistants on business trips and then danced with them all night, have you?"

"Just once." He saw the flash of disappointment in her eyes. "I'm kidding. I swear. I'm kidding."

"Are you sure we can work together and be…us?"

Ed stopped moving and just held her there. "Let's try. Please."

Darcy nodded. "The last relationship I was in was during my first year in college. I thought it was love, and I was so sadly mistaken. I'm not very good at trusting people."

He knew that about her just by the things she'd said about her own family. It wasn't that she didn't love them, but she was a little gun shy when it came to accepting things.

"Darcy, I'm not going to hurt you. My last three relationships weren't love either. I thought they were, but when I'm with you, I know I had no idea what I was thinking then."

She pushed back. "Are you saying you love me?"

Well, he hadn't said it in those words, but that was very much what he'd just said.

"If I said it to you, would you believe me?"

She quickly shook her head. "No. You can't think you love me already. So no."

"Then I won't say it."

She nodded nervously. "Thank you. I think I should get to bed."

"I'll walk you up."

"No. I don't trust this right now. I don't trust me. I'll meet you in the lobby at seven in the morning."

"Okay."

She turned to leave.

"Darcy." She turned back to him. "Sleep well."

CHAPTER 29

*W*hen the elevator doors began to close and she was headed to her room, alone, she knew things were slipping away from her.

She already knew she was in love with Ed Keller. Oh, who was she kidding? She was in love with the entire Keller family.

But she was living a huge lie. She hadn't meant to, but she was.

She'd come to Tennessee to find her birth parents. Her intention was to work her way into Benson, Benson, and Hart and do what she needed to do to find the people who gave her life.

It had been an honest coincidence to have fallen into the job. How much better could a plan work than to fall right into the arms of the man who could get her all the information she needed?

It had been a completely dishonest move to sit with Candy and look into the records. It had even been more wrong to have put in her own mind the thought that Zach and Mary Ellen had an affair.

Worse was, she'd believed it until Candy showed her that

Mary Ellen didn't have her baby until Darcy was nine months old.

She stepped off the elevator and walked to her room. It had been wrong to dishonor her mother's memory by searching for her birth mother.

Could guilt literally eat you up and kill you?

Darcy slipped the key card into the door and let herself into the room. She quickly changed out of her dress and pulled her hair back.

She turned on the TV and sat there mindlessly listening to the show that came on.

The thought crossed her mind. Ed Keller was in love with her.

She let out a breath. How crazy was that? This man—this powerful man—was in love with her. And if she was being honest with herself, which she decided she finally would be, she loved him.

The very thought made her stomach churn. Not because she loved him, but because she wasn't being honest with him.

She had to come clean. She had to tell him what she'd come to Tennessee for. If he decided she was deceitful and full of lies, he could send her packing.

Her breath came in spurts now.

Darcy could go back to Nashville and pack up her things. She could be back in Kentucky by the end of the week, and it would be as though nothing had transpired.

Nothing but the biggest opportunities of her life passing her by.

Darcy pressed her hand to her chest and tried to calm herself down.

If she felt the way she thought she did about Ed Keller, she owed him the truth. The charade was over.

. . .

Ed had just turned off the light when the pounding started on his door. He jumped out of bed, in only his boxers, and flung himself at the door.

There stood Darcy, in her pajamas with her hair pulled back. Her face was pale, and her teeth chattered as if she were freezing.

"Are you okay?" He pulled her in. "What on earth is wrong?"

"I have to come clean. I have to tell you what I've done."

Ed led her to the couch and sat her down. He went to the mini fridge and pulled out a bottle of water and twisted off the top before handing it to her.

"Calm down."

She took a sip as he sat down next to her.

Darcy sucked in a ragged breath and turned to look at him. "I didn't mean to run into you at Starbucks and spill my drink. I didn't know who you were. I swear."

Ed nodded. "I know that."

"Working in the firm wasn't in my plan for months. I'm not kidding. I thought I'd get there, but not like this."

"Things happen. It's okay." He had no idea what she was going on about, but she was shaking. "Darcy, what is this all about? I gave you the job because you were qualified."

Darcy shook her head and took another sip of the water.

"I hired a private investigator to help me find my birth parents."

"And they found them?"

She bit down on her lip. "I couldn't afford much. But he was able to tell me that it would lead me to Benson, Benson, and Hart."

Ed's brows drew in. "Who would be there?"

She shrugged. "I don't know. But," she dropped her shoulders and let out a breath, "I met someone who dug through some of the old files for me."

He stood and paced, not even caring that he was in his underwear. "Someone in my company helped you search for your birth parents?"

Darcy nodded.

He ran his fingers through his hair. "Who?"

"I'm not going to tell you that. It wasn't their fault. I convinced them to look. Please don't get mad."

"So all of this—us—this is just a sham to you to find your birth parents?"

"No." Darcy stood. "That's what I'm trying to tell you. I didn't mean to involve you at all."

"But it wouldn't have mattered if I hadn't fallen in love with you?"

She opened her mouth and then closed it again.

Ed rubbed the tension from his neck. "Did you find what you were looking for?"

"No," she said softly and looked at the ground. "I thought I knew, but I was wrong. I didn't find anything."

He nodded and then rested his hands on his hips, unsure what to do with them since he wasn't dressed. "Why are you telling me this? Why now?"

"Because I couldn't deceive you anymore. It was what drove me to Tennessee. And even when you left to come here, I thought I could get Curtis to help me find out about my birth mother from the hospital. But now it all seems wrong."

"Oh, you think?"

"Ed," she moved to him, but stopped short of reaching him. "That's why I'm here. I can't be in love with you and have lied to you."

"Now you're saying you're in love with me."

"I knew that I was in love with you. It's not that I didn't trust you." She looked down at the ground. "I didn't trust me."

He took the bottle of water from her and took a sip. His throat had suddenly gone very dry.

"Why would someone tell you that the path to your birth parents ended with BBH?"

"I don't know. That's all he told me. For all I know, he might have taken my money and found the company in some directory somewhere. But I can't go any further in this relationship without you knowing the truth. Until the moment you told me who you were, I honestly didn't know. I didn't seek you out to deceive you. I was only trying to find out who I was."

Ed set the bottle down on the coffee table and turned to her. He took her hands in his and looked her in the eye.

"You don't have to find those people to validate who you are. Maybe your mother and father had a reason for not telling you who gave you to them. Did you ever think they were protecting you from something?"

Her lip began to tremble. "No."

"Well, maybe you should trust them. It doesn't look like they made any mistakes with you, so why go searching? Why bother?"

Tears were forming in her eyes and threatening to fall. She tried to bat them away, but there were too many and they began stream down her cheeks.

"Please tell me you don't hate me. Please tell me you forgive me." She sniffed back her tears. "I'll leave. I'll go forever if that's what you want. But I needed you to know the truth, and now you do."

Ed kept his grip on her hands. He was furious that she'd go behind his back and search the company files. Even if he understood it, he didn't accept that. But everyone made mistakes.

What would he think if he were in her shoes? If he found out Madeline and Carlos Keller were not his parents, how would he feel?

He knew exactly how he'd feel—betrayed, just as Darcy felt.

"I'm very upset about this," he said. "I wish you'd just been honest with me. I would have helped you."

"I'm sorry."

Ed lifted his hand to her cheek and brushed away her tears with his thumb. "I'm going to say this, and then you can decide how you want to deal with it."

Darcy's eyes grew wide, but she nodded.

"I love you."

She choked back a sob. "Still?"

"I think forever."

Darcy moved in closer and wrapped her arms around him. "Please don't change your mind."

"Why would I?"

"I don't know. I'm scared."

Ed rested his cheek against the top of her head and pulled her close. "Don't be scared. I want this too much. I don't want to lose you."

Darcy shifted and looked up at him. "You can trust me. I want you to know that you can. That's why I had to come up here—now. You had to know."

CHAPTER 30

*D*arcy watched his eyes as he processed it all. He'd said he loved her, and she was going to run with that. Her father wasn't a man that said it easily or often, but when he did, he meant it. She had to assume that when Ed Keller said it, he meant it.

She'd been so wrapped up in telling him what she'd done that she hadn't realized just how insufficiently dressed they both were. Her bare arms pressed against his back and her face had been flush against his chest, where she could hear his heart beat in her ear.

A tank top and a pair of shorts were all that covered her, and he only had on a pair of boxers. This instant tantrum of hers had certainly thrown them into an interesting situation.

However, Ed Keller was much too much a gentleman to either have noticed or to ever take advantage of it.

"Darcy, I'd use every resource I have to find your birth parents. If that's what you want. I'd do that for you."

She sighed and shifted her arms so they encircled Ed's neck. His hands rested low on her hips as she rose up on her toes to look him eye to eye.

"Thank you, but I don't want to. I don't care anymore."

"You don't care?"

She shook her head. "My parents are Francis and George McCary. Whoever came before them…well, they didn't really have anything to do with me, did they?"

"You're sure about this?"

"Very sure. As far as I'm concerned now, the desire to find out simply led me right here." She pressed against him tighter. "Right into your arms. Otherwise…"

"Let's not think about otherwise," he said as he lowered his lips to hers and hoisted her up.

Darcy wrapped her legs around Ed's waist, and he carried her to the bed and laid her down.

His mouth was hot on hers, and his body pressed against hers. She'd never in her life felt so right about anything, but Ed's kisses stopped.

"What's wrong?" she asked, her own breath caught in her chest.

"How old fashioned are you?"

"I'm not." She wanted to laugh, but there'd been a seriousness to his voice. "Why?"

"Don't get me wrong. I could very much go through with this."

That much she already knew.

Ed lowered his forehead to hers and rested himself with his palms against the mattress. "Sleep in here with me. Stay in my bed, and let me wrap my arms around you all night."

"I will."

"For the rest of the week—you belong right here, with me."

"Okay."

Ed lowered himself down and rolled to her side. He scooped her against him and held her tight. "I'll make love to you some-day. For right now, I think I want to be a bit old fashioned."

She had to admit she was a bit let down. How could she possibly want this more than he did? That wasn't typical, was it?

But the soft gaze from his chocolate brown eyes said there was something different about this. This was compassion, respect —this was true love.

Every woman's dream was to find a man and wait for the moment to be right. To be that bride who made a wedding night special. Was this what Ed Keller was thinking? Was that his plan?

Panic erupted in her chest. Marriage?

They'd known each other for only a week. Finding the right person was one thing. Falling in love with them immediately was another, but this?

She cleared her mind. He hadn't said a word about getting married and there she was, her over active mind playing tricks on her again. One thing she knew, Ed Keller was a gentleman.

She rested her head against his chest and listened to his breathing slow.

"Ed."

"Yeah," his voice rumbled in his chest.

"Thank you. You could have tossed me out, and you didn't."

"I believe in second chances. My parents taught me that."

"You come from a long line of good people."

"That I do," he yawned. "Consider them your family, too. They've really taken to you. That says a lot about your character."

Darcy closed her eyes. To be part of the Keller family was a dream she didn't know she'd ever wanted until that day she'd bumped into Ed. Fate was a strange thing. But it seemed to be on her side.

CHAPTER 31

*W*aking up wrapped in Ed's arms made the week worth of meetings tolerable. Darcy had no idea insurance was so boring.

As she and Ed sat on the wall of a planter just down the block from the construction site, eating hot dogs from a cart, she realized how happy she was.

Things were just as she'd always assumed they'd be when she realized she was in love. The sun was brighter. People were cheerier. And there was a peace that resonated through her.

Ed had kept his word. They had shared a bed for the past three nights, and a million kisses too, but he never pushed the limit to where they couldn't stop themselves. He was absolutely a breath of fresh air.

Ed bit into his hot dog and looked around. "I think we should be done here by tomorrow."

"Should I arrange our flight?"

He nodded as he took in the scenery. "Yeah, let's make that a plan. It's time to head home."

Darcy bit down on her hot dog and then quickly wiped away the ketchup that dripped down her chin. "I want you to know that I understand your position in the company, too. I'm not going to flaunt our relationship around in the office. And by no means do I expect anything special."

Ed nodded and sipped from his soda can. "I am beginning to think you're worried about working for me, back in the office that is."

"It's not playing out right in my head."

"I don't see any problems with it."

She knew she was making a bigger deal out of it, but she couldn't help herself. "Tell me again why your uncle fired your aunt."

He laughed. "You are worried, aren't you?"

"They seem perfectly happy, that's all."

"They are perfectly happy."

"They why would he ever have fired her?"

Ed drank down the last sip of his drink and then crushed the can. "Like I said, it wasn't really that she did anything."

"You said she'd lost him a contract."

Ed wadded up the paper his hot dog had come in. Something about the subject she'd brought up was making him uncomfortable.

After a few moments of silence, he took a deep breath and dropped his shoulders. "My aunt was involved with a man long before my uncle. I didn't know him. None of us did. In fact, I really don't remember anything about her being with him. They lived in Hawaii, and then he tried to kill her."

"He tried to kill her?" She nearly choked on her words. "Why would he do something like that? What kind of monster tries to kill someone as wonderful as your aunt?"

Ed shook his head. "I don't know. I told you, I don't really know anything about all this. She came back and was in the hospital. But my parents kept us far from all that. I didn't see Aunt Regan for months after she moved back to Nashville."

"Maybe they were afraid he'd come after her family."

Ed nodded. "Well, they did tell him that she had died."

Darcy covered her mouth. "Why would they…"

"So he'd go away." He shook his head. "I know it was wrong, but it was the first thing Curtis could think to do. But the man found out that she was alive and came back after her…after her family."

Darcy reached for him. "Did he hurt her? Did he hurt you?"

"No. Not me, but he started stalking Arianna and," he cleared his throat. Something had choked him up. "He knocked my sister around."

A tear escaped Darcy's eye. This wasn't at all what she'd expected to hear. "Ed, I'm so sorry."

"Anyway, he tried to kill John. Knocked him cold and then went after Clara, Arianna, and Regan. He cornered them into her theater and set it on fire."

The tears streamed down her face now, but there was no wiping them away. "But they're okay. They're all okay?"

This time Ed smiled. "Have you ever met three more stubborn, more amazing women in your life?" He clasped his hands together. "In the chaos of the fire, Regan was able to grab hold of the gun in Arianna's purse."

"Oh." She let the word breathe out on her exhaled breath. "She…"

"Yeah, she shot and killed him." He dropped his shoulders. "No one knows the story quite like that, so I'd appreciate if you kept it to yourself. I don't know why I told you."

That stung. "I'm hoping you thought you could trust me since you've said you love me." Her words were curt, but what did he think?

Darcy lowered her defenses. What else would he think? She'd started their relationship on a lie—no wonder he'd worry that she'd spread some rumor.

"Darcy, it's not that I don't trust you." He ran his hand over her head. "That man hurt a lot of people. That whole subject has been dead and buried for almost twenty years. It's just something better forgotten."

She nodded quickly. One thing about being an only child, and a protected one at that, she needed to learn that everything wasn't about her. This was about Ed's family—his entire family.

She understood now that Zach hadn't fired Regan just out of spite. There was more, so much more.

Darcy reached for Ed's hand. "Thank you for sharing that with me."

"Are you quite convinced that I won't fire you yet?"

"No, but I will certainly keep my nose clean. I promise."

He leaned in and kissed her softly. "C'mon, let's get this paperwork all wrapped up so we can head home."

CHAPTER 32

*D*arcy had never been so glad to board an airplane in her life. If she never had to talk to another insurance person again, it would be too soon.

But the important part was that Benson, Benson, and Hart's reputation was still intact, and Valerie's company was able to stay in business, even if it was their steel that had nearly killed someone.

As the plane touched down in Tennessee, Darcy turned on her phone, and it beeped with a voicemail almost immediately.

It was a message from her aunt asking her to call as soon as she could.

"Do you think everything is alright?" Ed reached for her hand and gave it a squeeze.

"I don't know. My aunt lives in Florida. I can't imagine why..." She felt the blood drain from her face. "What if something happened to my father?"

"We'll call the moment we exit the plane."

Ed had pulled her to a bank of chairs as soon as they were clear of the walkway. Darcy sat down and dialed her aunt's number.

"Aunt Carol, is something wrong?"

"Your father had an accident, but he's okay," she was quick to add. "He hit his head, and he's in the hospital. But they're letting him go today, and Uncle Tom and I are headed his way."

"I'll be there when you get there."

"Don't you go being silly. You have things going on. Your daddy told me you got a good job, and you're making your own way now."

Darcy's eyes stung from the tears that welled up in them. "I am, but I'll be there. I want to make sure he's okay."

"Darcy Ann, if you show up there you make sure you tell him I told you to stay put. You know that old fart. He'll blame me."

Darcy laughed through her tears. "I'll be sure to tell him. I'll see you soon."

She disconnected the call and stared down at her phone.

Ed slipped his arm around her shoulders. "Is everything okay?"

She nodded. "I need to go home for a few days."

"Whatever you need."

"He hit his head, and he's in the hospital."

"But she said he's okay?"

"Yes." She swallowed hard. "He's in his seventies and diabetic. Ed, what if he shouldn't be by himself? What if my mom being gone and my leaving set him into some kind of downward spiral?"

"You said he was a doctor, right?"

"Yes."

"Then wouldn't he know if something was wrong?"

Darcy knew that her father would never neglect his health or let his diabetes get out of control.

"You're right." She tucked the phone back in her purse and looked around. "I need to get on the next flight to Kentucky."

"I'll help you get that situated."

. . .

ED HAD BEEN MORE THAN GRACIOUS TO SIT WITH HER AND WAIT until her flight had been called. He'd even paid for her ticket, which she'd wished he hadn't done.

She had, however, talked him into only buying a one-way ticket. Perhaps now that she knew her way around town, she could convince her father to let her use her mother's car, which sat abandoned in the garage, and she could drive it back. She'd feel better if she had her own transportation.

As she flew out of Nashville, Darcy leaned her head against the seat and thought of the things Ed had told her about his aunt. She couldn't imagine a woman loving a man who was that hateful. What had Regan seen in someone like that, she wondered?

But wasn't it funny how things always worked out? Even her own father had been married before he married her mother. Oh, it had been a short-lived marriage to a woman, a nurse, who was also in the Army. She'd never asked him about her. Maybe now she would.

It gave her a moment of concern though. If her father had once remarried—and even Ed's parents had once divorced and remarried, and then remarried each other—was Ed the man for her? Or was he a stepping stone in her life?

Oh, she certainly didn't want to think like that. Was it possible to love the first man you truly knew in your heart was the right one? What if she'd made a mistake and missed the transitional person? What if she'd bypassed the right path when she bumped into him in Starbucks.

A bead of sweat trickled down her back.

You could make your own destiny, right? Isn't that what her mother always told her?

And then, as if her mother had touched her shoulder, Darcy understood that very saying.

In a moment of uncertainty, Darcy had hired that investigator to help her find herself. He'd led her to Tennessee, where in fact she had found herself.

Ed Keller wasn't just something that happened along. It was part of the destiny that Darcy was supposed to have. She was supposed to be part of the Keller family, and she was supposed to meet the man of her dreams while she was covered in a coffee drink.

When the plane touched down in Kentucky, she'd be able to actually tell her father that she had everything she'd ever wanted and that she was happy. That's all he'd ever wanted for her.

The pain in her heart, from learning she was adopted and from her mother passing, was easing. Ed Keller would never treat her the way that man treated Regan. He hadn't even made a move to have sex with her. This was the kind of gentleman her father would approve of.

It was all going to be okay. This new life she'd made in Nashville was the life she was meant to have.

CHAPTER 33

*W*hen the plane landed in Ashland, Darcy collected her things and headed off the plane. It was a funny feeling, flying back. Usually when she'd walk through the airport, there was a feeling of coming home, but that wasn't the case this time. Could Nashville have become her home so quickly?

When she collected her bags, she climbed into the taxi and told the driver to take her to King's Daughters Medical Center. Oh, her father was going to be livid.

And he proved that he was the moment she walked into his room.

"You shouldn't be here. Oh, that sister of mine can't keep her big mouth shut, can she?"

Darcy set her suitcase on the floor and walked to the bed where her father sat. His head was bandaged and he had an IV in his arm, but other than that, he looked perfectly fine.

"It's nice to see you too, Daddy."

The smile he'd tried to keep hidden under the frown snuck through. "Did you spend all your savings just to come home and make sure my head was still attached? Just a few stitches, that's all."

"Then why did they keep you overnight?"

His brows furrowed. "Blood sugar."

Darcy nodded. That was what she figured. "Did they say when you could go home?"

"When someone came to get me. But what about Carol? She was coming for me."

"I presume she's on her way. I happened to be at the airport when I heard you were here. I jumped on another flight, and here I am."

Her father growled. "What did your boss think about that?"

"He bought my ticket."

"Sounds like a nice man."

"That he is." She tapped her fingertips against her thigh and moved closer to her father's bed. "Maybe we should call for a nurse so we can take you home."

DARCY WAS A BIT SURPRISED WHEN SHE WALKED THROUGH THE front door of the house she'd grown up in. There were no more pictures on the walls, and the hallway was lined with cardboard boxes.

"Daddy, what's going on in here?" she asked as he walked ahead of her and into the kitchen.

"I'm moving."

"Were you going to discuss this with me?"

"Darcy, you left me. Remember? You moved on with your life, and don't you suppose I should be able to do the same?"

"Sure. I just thought maybe you'd mention it first."

Her father took a glass from the cupboard and filled it with water. He then took the bottle of pills they'd given him from his pocket, opened them, and swallowed one back.

"Your mother is gone. This is no more my home any more than that hospital bed was."

Darcy ran her hand over a stack of papers on the kitchen table. "What are you going to do?"

"Aunt Carol says the community where she lives is a nice place." He shrugged and set the glass in the sink. "She's the only family I have left, besides you. I should spend the rest of my time with my family, don't you think?"

She was sure guilt could eat you up and kill you quickly.

"I could move home," she said, but her voice wavered.

Her father laughed. "You think I'd ask you to do that?"

"No."

"You're right." He walked to the table, pulled out a chair, and sat down. "Sit."

Darcy did as she was told.

Her father reached across the table and took her hands. "I'm proud of you, Darcy Ann. It took a lot of guts to pack up and move."

"Daddy…"

"Don't interrupt me."

She dropped her shoulders. Adult or not, this man could quickly put her in her place.

"Your job. It's a good one, right?"

"Yes."

"Your boss. You said he's a nice man."

"Yes."

Her father narrowed his eyes. "Did you find your birth parents yet?"

Darcy was sure her heart had fallen out of her chest and just been stomped into the ground. She pulled her hands from her father's and cupped them around her mouth to keep the sobs that were about to escape from doing so.

Her father stood and walked to the paper towel roll which hung by the sink. He pulled down the roll and handed the whole thing to her. She pulled off a sheet and began frantically wiping away her tears as he sat back down.

"I knew that telling you that you were adopted would lead to that. I'm not stupid, you know."

All Darcy could do was nod.

"I don't know who they were. We didn't deal with them directly. It was set up through the hospital. I don't think the father was involved."

Darcy looked up at her father. He was feeding her information. Would he always just have done that?

He scratched his head, and then, as if he'd just noticed it, he pulled the gauze strip from his arm and wadded up the bandage. "You were born early. I think about six weeks early. There had been some kind of accident or something, and we were told your mother died."

The sobs broke through, and Darcy pulled off more of the paper towel and began to wipe at her face.

Her father looked down at his hands. "You were in NICU for three weeks, fighting for your life. We figured it was just a cruel joke that the world was playing on us. When we finally got the call that there was a baby for us, there was a chance she was going to die."

"I never knew that."

"There was no need for you to know." He rubbed his hand over the stubble on his chin. "If the woman who had you was dead and you'd survived, why make you even think about it?"

"That's why you didn't tell me?"

He shrugged. "We didn't see any reason."

How could she possibly deny him that logic.

"I love you. I love both of you. I should never have gone looking for my birth parents. But…" she paused as she contemplated what she was going to say. "Had I not tried, I'd never have fallen in love with the most wonderful man."

Her father clasped his hands and then looked down at them. This was something he'd do before he got very angry. Darcy placed her hands in her lap and waited.

And waited.

Soon her father stood from his seat and walked out of the house. Darcy sat there for a few more minutes, but he never returned.

Finally she walked outside where her father was putting boxes into the back of his pickup truck.

"Are you moving right now?" she asked as she walked down the front steps of the house.

"No. You are."

"Dad, how hard did you hit your head?"

He laughed. "Not hard at all. You're taking my truck and all this crap your mother saved for you. She collected dishes, linens, picture frames, and hell, I don't know what else. She boxed them and marked them with your name for twenty years. They were for when you got married, so you might as well take them."

"I'm not getting married."

"You just told me you were in love."

"Well, yes."

"Then I would expect if he is a decent man, he'd be asking you to marry him."

She moved closer to the truck. "I would expect that he would someday, too. But this is a new relationship."

Her father threw the last box into the back of the truck and looked at her. "Who is he? Who is this man who has taken your heart?"

He was so unsentimental that when he said that she almost burst out laughing.

"Eduardo Keller."

Her father pursed his lips. "And what does this Eduardo man do?"

Darcy cleared her throat. "He is the Vice President of Benson, Benson, and Hart."

Her father pushed up the tailgate and stood there with his arms folded on it. "You're having an affair with your boss?"

"No. It's not like that."

"Not how I hear it."

"Daddy, I'm not like that. You know that."

"Maybe Nashville has changed you." He walked past her and back into the house.

This time she followed. "Do you really think of me like that?"

"Darcy, you always took your own path."

"No, I didn't. I did all the things I was supposed to do. I never strayed off course—ever. I got straight A's. I won trophies in every sport I ever played. I graduated from college. What more was I supposed to do?"

He shook his head. "I don't know." He walked to the living room and sat down in his recliner. "I know it's been a year, Darcy, but I miss your mother."

Darcy let out a loud sigh and dropped her shoulders. "Is this what it's all about? Are you really just missing her? Or are you really mad at me?"

He shook his head. "I'm proud of you. I really am."

"That's all I've ever tried to do is make you proud. Daddy," she said as she knelt down in front of him. "I love Ed. He's a hard-working man, and he has this amazing family."

"A big family?"

"Yes!" She laughed when she said it. "And they are all so kind. You're going to love them."

He grunted.

"Daddy, why don't you come with me. If Ashland isn't home anymore to either of us because Mom is gone, then come with me."

This time he laughed. "Are you kidding me? Nashville isn't for me. Trust me."

"So you're going to move to Florida? You're going to go and be happy there?"

He ran his tongue over his teeth. "I'm going to try, honey. I was happy with your mother."

The sentiment choked her, and she moved to him, wrapping her arms around his neck. That statement took a lot for him to say. She knew that.

"Well then," she said and then kissed him on the cheek, "how can I help you get ready for your move?"

CHAPTER 34

*D*arcy listened to the rumble of the truck as she drove away from her father's house. He waved from the porch and then blew her a kiss.

She never would have imagined she'd be driving away in his truck—his precious "as old as Kentucky" truck.

When she got to the first stop light, she dialed the now familiar number on her cell phone. Her heart kicked up a notch when Ed answered.

"Please tell me you're on your way home and everything is okay."

Darcy laughed. "I'm on my way home and everything is okay."

Ed let out a breath into the phone. "Are you flying in? Or did you get your mom's car?"

"He gave me his pickup. This one will put your truck to shame."

This time, Ed laughed. "I can't wait to see it."

"I'll be there in about five hours, unless I stop."

"Don't stop. I miss you."

Could everything have worked out any better? "I'll hurry."

"So, you'll be home before eight then. If you're not too tired, how about I take you out for a drink?"

"A drink? Don't you just want to come over and hang out? My dad sent me home with a whole bunch of stuff that my mom saved for the past twenty-four years."

"Though that sounds like fun, Clara is playing with Randy Seymour at The Commodore tonight. I thought we'd go see her show."

There was a stream of pride that echoed in his voice.

"I wouldn't miss it for the world. I'll be there soon."

"Okay," he said. "Be careful, and remember, I love you."

Darcy sighed. "I love you, too."

DARCY PULLED THE TRUCK UP BEHIND THE HOUSE AND PARKED next to Christian's car. He obviously hadn't driven since he'd been hurt. His windshield looked as though it had been abused by birds. It gave her a chuckle.

Before she unloaded her truck, she'd pop her head in to see how Christian was feeling.

He was standing at the sink, balanced on his crutches, shirtless with only a pair of lounge pants on. She figured it was better than the towel she'd seen him in.

"How are you feeling?" she asked.

"Like crap. I'm done being immobile."

Darcy nodded. "What did they say about your leg then? Isn't it healing?"

He gave her a shrug. "Looks like surgery for me."

"I'm sorry."

He let out a snort. "Just figures. I thought I had a shot at the show this time. But before I even get started, I'm a washed-up has-been."

"Christian, this happens to players all the time. Keep a positive outlook."

"Right. Positive. Maybe some other day."

Darcy could certainly understand his anger, but she hated to see him so upset.

"When are they talking surgery?"

"Second week of August with a follow up around the twenty-first."

She felt the smile form on her lips. "Ah, good day."

"Why is that?"

"My birthday."

His face softened. "Good. I'll be ready to celebrate something good by then."

"Can I get you anything?" she asked as she turned toward the door.

"Nah." He looked out the window. "Did you get yourself some new wheels? Or at least find some old wheels on the side of the road? How old is that truck?"

Darcy laughed. "My father gave me his cherished truck. It's a sixty-nine or seventy, I think."

"Holy cow."

"It'll get me around."

"Well, when I'm back on both feet, maybe I can help you fix it up. She could be a beauty."

Darcy liked that. A project with a brother—that was something she'd never had the chance to do. Never in her life did she think she wanted to fix up an old truck, but looking at the enthusiasm in Christian's eyes, she wanted to now.

"Sounds like a plan. Well, yell if you need anything. I guess we're going to go watch Clara tonight."

"Yeah, I'll be going with you. I suppose I should get ready. It might take me that long."

"I'll come up in a bit."

With that, she walked out the back door and down to her apartment.

. . .

Ed pulled up in front of the house shortly before eight. It seemed strange that he'd have to pick his brother and his girl-friend up at the same house. He'd give that some thought. Maybe it was time to change the living arrangements. Darcy should live with him, not with Christian.

That was a bit possessive, he decided as he climbed out of his truck. He didn't like feeling that way. Besides, dating a woman after a few weeks of knowing her was one thing—moving in together was something much different.

As Ed climbed out of his truck, the front door opened and there stood Darcy. She was a sight.

There was urgency in his step, but he fought himself from running up the front steps. He didn't want to seem desperate.

"You look beautiful," he said as he reached the porch.

"Why, thank you." She let the screen door shut behind her as she walked to the edge of the porch and waited for him to walk up the steps.

Her jeans hung to her hips, giving her a curvy, sexy look. The lacy top she wore was very feminine. Ed liked that. Her dark hair fell just to her shoulders, but she had added some curl. This casual and fun look had his blood warming.

Ed took the last step up to the porch and stood looking down into her dark eyes.

Darcy took his hands in hers and intertwined their fingers. "I know it's only been a few days since I've seen you, but it seems like forever," she said as she moved in closer to him.

"I couldn't agree more."

She rose up on her toes to place a kiss against his lips, but a simple peck wasn't going to hold him until later. It had been hours—days—since he'd tasted her kisses, and he wasn't going to wait a moment longer.

Ed released her hands and wrapped his arms around her waist, pulling her as close to him as he could. She let out a grunt, but quickly eased back into the kiss he was sinking them both with.

If he hadn't promised his sister he'd be there...

"Would you two knock it off out there? This is a reputable neighborhood," Christian's voice broke through the silence of their kiss.

Ed rested his head against Darcy's. "Do we have to take him?"

"Yes, you have to take me," Christian said, standing just inside the door. "Get me out of this house before I lose my mind."

Ed chuckled. "I'm beginning to get used to you on crutches."

"Yeah, well, I'd rather be crouched down behind a batter, but..."

Ed realized by Christian's attitude that he was feeling extremely down on himself.

Christian was the sensitive type. He liked a good time, but Christian was a gentleman to the extreme. It wasn't like him to be snappy, so Ed knew he could use a night out.

"I suppose you're going to call shotgun, too?" Ed snapped back at him.

"I'd ride in the back of that stupid truck if it meant I didn't have to sit here all night."

Ed chuckled. "C'mon then, Clara will be looking for us."

CHAPTER 35

The Commodore already had a decent size crowd when they arrived.

"Clara said she had a table for us all up front," Ed said as he led them toward the stage.

Darcy wasn't sure why she was surprised to find the entire Keller clan there. That seemed to be a given, no matter what anyone of them did.

Each of them stood, and the men shook Ed's hand and the women kissed his cheeks. But when each of them hugged her and kissed her as well, tears began to sting the back of her throat.

Regan looked at her. "Are you okay?"

"I'm getting used to this big family stuff."

Regan smiled. "You are family. You mean everything to Ed, so you mean everything to us."

Her words tugged at Darcy's heart. What was it about Regan Benson that made the world right?

Darcy took her seat and listened to the banter that went back and forth between them all. She was a part of this family. That gave her as much pride and joy as being a McCary.

A man walked on stage and announced the performance for the evening. It was just what the crowd had wanted to hear.

"Randy is a friend that Clara used to write songs with. He's getting a lot of attention lately," Ed leaned in and said in her ear.

She nodded. "I think I've heard of him."

"You're going to be hearing a lot more. This guy is going to be famous."

There was that Keller pride in the smile that Ed wore. "What about Clara? She's very comfortable up there."

He shrugged. "She just loves to play and sing."

And that was exactly how she saw her when Clara stood in front of the mic and the duo began to entertain. Clara was comfortable being Clara.

Darcy looked around the table. Pride radiated from the group, and even Darcy felt it. But as Regan had said, she was part of this family. Clara was as close to a sister as she could imagine, but then the moment of clarity hit. She was a part of this family as long as she was on Ed's arm. What if this thing with Ed didn't work out? What if, in the end, Darcy just became an employee of Benson, Benson, and Hart—or worse—an ex-employee?

The warmth in the room began to chill. Her body began to shake, and Ed had taken note.

"Are you sure you're okay?"

"I'm perfect, and that's what's wrong."

Her voice had cracked when she said it, and he leaned in closer to her.

"How can that be wrong?"

"What if it goes away?"

There was an understanding that surfaced in his dark eyes. "I'm not going anywhere, Darcy. I'm yours—forever."

That was even more nerve wracking. Forever. Oh, she was quite comfortable with it. She was the daughter of two people who had been married nearly fifty years. They were very in love. Her mother was a nurturer and her father the protector. She understood forever. She just never thought forever would come so quickly after she found the right man—or ran in to him.

Darcy stood from her seat, and Ed stood, too.

"Where are you going?"

"I'm going to the ladies' room. I just need a moment."

Darcy grabbed her purse and headed off.

She pushed the door open to the restroom and was happy to see that there weren't very many people in there. She wasn't sure if she just needed to breathe or cry.

A moment later, the door opened and in walked Madeline.

What could have been worse?

"Ed's worried about you."

Darcy tried to be calm, but this was the woman who was the least likely to like her if things went wrong. Though, she couldn't see Madeline Keller disliking anyone.

"I'm okay. After having been with my father, I'm just trying to embrace the enormous size of your family. I'm sorry if I seem a bit out of sorts."

Madeline smiled. "Your father is okay? Ed said he was in the hospital."

Darcy nodded. "Just a bump on his head. I call it military stubborn. He thinks he can fight anything—or anyone."

That made Madeline laugh. "He sounds like a good man."

He was, and at that moment, Darcy's chest swelled with pride. Those two people who had given her a name and a life were just that—good people.

"He is a good man. And my mother..." she choked out before the first tear rolled down her cheek, "she was amazing."

"Ed and Christian told me she died of cancer."

Darcy wasn't comfortable talking about the disease that had stolen her mother from her and had threatened to take Madeline, too.

"Yes. It was quick. She was diagnosed and gone within a year."

Madeline shook her head and rested her hand on her chest.

"I'm so sorry. I know that when I had cancer the part that hurt the worst was wondering if I'd see my children grow up."

Darcy nodded and wiped her eyes. "I feel even worse because before she was diagnosed they had finally told me I was adopted."

"That's a lot to have to absorb. But, I must say, you're in the right place if you want support being an adopted child."

Darcy smiled. "So I've heard."

Madeline opened the door to a stall, pulled off a handful of toilet paper, and handed it to Darcy.

"Thank you."

Madeline rested against the sink counter and folded her arms in front of her. "So, about you and Ed…"

Darcy felt the heat rise in her cheeks. Here it came. The I don't think you're good enough for my son talk. She braced herself.

"He tells me he's in love with you."

Darcy nearly choked on a sob. "He said that to you?"

"My children and I are very close."

Darcy knew that. She wasn't sure how to answer so she only nodded.

Madeline smiled. "I think Christian is disappointed, but only because he likes to give his brother a run for his money."

That made Darcy laugh through her tears.

Madeline reached for her and rested her hands on Darcy's arms. "Ed isn't one to tell me he loves someone when he doesn't. When he knows what he wants, he goes after it, and he usually gets what he wants."

That sounded about right.

Madeline pulled Darcy to her and wrapped her in the comfort of her motherly embrace. "I'd be thrilled to have you as part of my family."

Oh, God! The tears threatened again.

Madeline pulled back. "So, everything is okay?"

Darcy sucked back the last of her tears. "Everything is perfect."

Darcy walked back to her seat with Madeline, who had wrapped her arm around her shoulders as they approached the table.

Clara and Randy's voices echoed over the crowd. They had great sound and that pride she'd seen on the faces of Clara's family vibrated in Darcy's chest.

Ed stood as they headed back to him, and Madeline gave her shoulders a squeeze and then walked back toward Carlos.

"Everything okay? I didn't mean to send my mother in after you. She just…"

Darcy flung her arms around his neck and shut him up with a kiss. She was quickly learning it was very effective.

Ed looked over his shoulder at his extended family, who all turned their heads as if they hadn't been watching.

"You have a wonderful mother," Darcy said.

"I always thought so."

"Thank you for letting me have a moment with her. Now," she looked out at the dance floor, "you still owe me a dance."

Ed wasn't sure what his mother had said to Darcy, but he'd never seen such happiness in her eyes. This, most certainly, was the woman of his dreams, and he had every intention of keeping her.

With his sister's voice in his ears and the woman of his dreams in his arms, Ed gave some thought to something his brother had shared with him. Her birthday was only a few weeks away. Christian had made sure to mention it. He supposed stranger things had happened in the world than for a man to decide that, after only a few short weeks, he had found the woman he wanted to spend the rest of his life with. Curtis and Simone, after all, didn't get married until Avery was born. In fact, they'd gotten pregnant before they even fell in love.

His parents loved each other so much that divorce and marriage to others couldn't keep them apart.

Then there was the strange coincidence of his meeting Darcy in much the same way that his aunt and uncle met. Love happened when it was right, not when the people involved were ready.

Well, he was ready. The plan was in his head. This woman was going to be his—forever. And he'd ask her to make that her plan, too, on her birthday. Yes, he'd bring this family together again to celebrate the day she was born, and he'd ask her to be his wife. Nothing would make him happier, and nothing could possibly ruin such a wonderful plan.

CHAPTER 36

Something had changed that night when Darcy danced with Ed to his sister's music. He'd taken her home with him, and she'd slept in his arms, just as they had in Saint Louis. The best part about this wonderful love affair they were having—it was actually love.

Sex hadn't woven its way in and ruined what was absolutely a wonderful connection. Though, even Darcy wondered if he'd ever make a move.

Their kisses had become more passionate. Their caresses more desperate. At some point, one of them was going to crack, but Eduardo Keller seemed to have a steel trap for a mind, and like his mother said, when he made his mind up about something that was how it was going to be.

Darcy couldn't even begin to argue that. What kind of man made the choice to wait to make love to the woman he professed to love? A man like Ed Keller, that's who.

Darcy sat at her desk and looked over his schedule. He'd be traveling soon, and he'd be gone for a week. Then again for a few days. Of course, there was time marked on his schedule to be at the hospital with Christian for his routine surgery. She was sure someone could be with him, but if she knew the Keller family, and she was learning that she did know them already very well, they'd all be there.

The part that bothered her was that on her birthday he had marked an official meeting.

She hadn't made any comment to him about her birthday coming up. In fact, other than mentioning the date to Christian in conjunction with his follow-up surgery appointment, she hadn't mentioned it to anyone. But it would have been nice to spend the day with him.

"Darcy, can you come in here for a moment?" Ed's voice came through the intercom on her phone.

She picked up her note pad and headed into the office.

"I need to plan a trip to Florida next week," he said without looking up from his work.

"You're marked out for your brother's surgery."

"I know, but he'll have enough people there to take care of him. If I didn't tell him, he probably wouldn't know I wasn't there."

Darcy made the note on her pad. "Where exactly do I need to make your reservations for?"

"Miami."

She nodded. Would it be too bold to ask if she could go with him, just to see her father? He was right outside Miami. It wouldn't interfere with his business at all.

She took a breath to ask, but he interrupted her thoughts. "Mom knows I'm going, and she's glad you'll be around to help out Christian when he gets home."

Darcy let her shoulders drop. That was what family was all about, and she'd been told by numerous people that she was, indeed, part of this family.

"I'd be happy to help him out."

"Good." Ed finally looked up at her. "We're free for a few hours, aren't we?"

"You have a conference call at three."

"Let's go get some lunch."

Ed noticed that Darcy was extremely quiet as they drove to lunch. That was okay. He wasn't going to let her know why he was headed to Miami.

She'd made his airline reservation and booked him a hotel. From what he knew of the area, that would put him within twenty minutes of her father and aunt.

All he could hope for now was that her father wouldn't tell Darcy that he was coming to visit. He was sure her father knew what the visit was about. He sounded very bright when Ed had talked to him on the phone. But some things you just didn't do on the phone. If you were going to ask a man for his daughter's hand in marriage, you went to him—even if you had to fly to Miami to do it.

Ed reached for Darcy's hand and laced their fingers together. "You're quiet."

"Sorry. I have been thinking of my dad since you said you were headed to Miami."

"Oh, that's right. He lives near there, right?"

She nodded.

It put an ache in his chest to see her obvious pain of missing him, but he had to keep his plans.

"How about we go out there after your birthday?"

Darcy's head snapped up. "How do you know my birthday is coming up?"

"Christian mentioned it."

She nodded again. "He has an appointment that day."

"Right. Well, how about that weekend we fly out? Interested?"

"Really? You'd go out and meet my dad?"

"I think it would only be right, don't you?"

She smiled. "It would mean a great deal to me."

"Me too." He gave her hand a squeeze. Now his heart could ease up. But by the time they went out to visit, they'd be engaged with his blessing.

CHAPTER 37

*E*d left the next morning, and the office was quiet. Darcy had plenty of work to do, but it was always nicer when Ed was in the office behind her.

Zach and Mary Ellen had included her in their lunch plans, but she wasn't sure that she was comfortable, considering the thoughts she'd had about the couple. They had no idea what she'd led herself to believe, but she didn't want to chance looking like an idiot in front of them either.

Instead, she spent lunch in the Starbucks where she'd met Ed.

As she watched the people come and go, she wondered if anyone else would walk through the door and have their lives changed as she had, just weeks earlier. She came to Nashville in search of her birth parents, and instead, she became part of a family and fell in love with a man that she hoped she'd spend the rest of her life with.

When the door opened again, she couldn't have been more pleased than to see Clara's face.

Clara waved, ordered her drink, and then quickly hurried toward her with her arms out.

Darcy stood and hugged Ed's sister.

"Does he know you hide out in the coffee shop while he's out of town?" Clara laughed.

"Not a lot gets past him."

"That's for sure."

Clara's name was called, and she walked to the counter to fetch her drink.

"Can I join you?"

"Of course." Darcy sat back down, and Clara joined her.

She loosened the scarf around her neck, which must have been hot considering the heat they'd been having.

Clara was a free spirit, and anyone would know that just by looking at her. Her dark hair grazed just at her shoulders, and today, it was full of curls. She wore a pair of cut-off shorts, a sleeveless white shirt, and worn out cowboy boots. Darcy admired her unique fashion. She was a breath of fresh air with a wrist full of bangles.

Darcy noticed a tattoo on her wrist. "What's on your wrist?"

Clara turned her arm over and moved the bracelets so that it could be seen.

"It's the infinity symbol with the word family."

The very sentiment nearly brought tears to Darcy's eyes.

Clara ran her fingers over it. "We all have one."

"You all have one? As in who?"

"My family. Mom, Dad, Christian, and Ed."

Darcy tried to think. Had she seen his tattoo? No, she hadn't.

Clara let her bracelets fall back in place and took a sip of her drink. "We all decided when Mom got her bill of clean health that we wanted to commemorate that journey. We are a tight family, and we always will be. Even when Mom and Dad weren't married, we were tighter than most families."

"I've never seen Ed's tattoo."

Clara smiled. "I thought you guys were close—if you know what I mean."

Darcy could feel the heat rise in her cheeks. "Oh no, we've...I mean, we don't..."

Clara sat back in her seat and crossed her legs. "You mean to tell me you sleep in the same bed and don't do anything—but sleep?"

"Yes."

Clara bit down on her lip. "You really are the perfect girl, aren't you?"

Darcy wasn't sure if she should be put out by the accusation or pleased. "Between us, we've decided to wait."

"I think that's awesome."

"You do?"

Clara nodded as she sipped her coffee. "It means it's not the most important thing to you. Too many relationships start off with it and then..."

Darcy nodded. She understood that. She assumed her own beginnings might have started like that, too.

She took a sip of her coffee and looked back up at Clara. "Where are everyone else's tattoos?" She had to ask. She thought she'd seen almost all of Ed, and the number of times she'd seen Christian in nothing but a towel, she thought she would have noticed it.

"Dad has his on his shoulder. Mom has hers over her heart." She indicated the very place with her hand. "Christian's is inter-mixed with the barbed wire around his right arm."

Darcy gave some thought to the tattoo. She knew it well enough, but she'd never seen the symbol. Clara lifted her arm and pointed to the underside. Darcy nodded. That made sense.

"What about Ed?"

Clara laughed. "Well, it's just proof that you haven't been naked with the man." She leaned in closer to Darcy. "It's on his lower stomach over his appendix scar."

"That's a funny place for a family tattoo."

Clara sat back with her smile and looked her over. "Not if

you're the picture-perfect professional, and you don't want anyone to see it, no matter what."

"So it's hidden, but there?"

"Right."

Oh, now she knew she'd have to see it.

She looked down at her phone and noted the time. "I should get back upstairs. I have a conference call meeting with Ed and Zach."

"I certainly don't envy you. But tell him and Mary Ellen hello."

"I will."

"Isn't she the nicest person you've ever met?"

"She's taken very good care of me." She gave some thought about asking about her. "She and Zach were never a couple before he met your aunt, were they?"

"Mary Ellen and Zach?" The question made her laugh. "No."

"They're just very comfortable together."

"They should be. I think they've worked together for thirty-some years. Mary Ellen was there when Zach got his first desk. They grew up in the company, if you will. But he's always collected nice women as his dearest friends. Aunt Simone was his best friend from boarding school in Paris."

Darcy narrowed her eyes. "And she said he never had eyes for him."

Clara nodded. "No. He never wanted anything to do with her in that sense. It was almost like he knew Regan would come along."

"Fall into his lap."

"Ah, you do know the story."

Yes, she'd become very familiar with it.

Clara reached out her hand and covered Darcy's. "I'm glad you ran into Ed. I look forward to having you for a sister."

There was a lump forming in Darcy's throat now. She wanted that too—almost too much.

. . .

DARCY SAT AT THE TABLE WITH MARY ELLEN AND ZACH. WHEN the call came through and she heard Ed's voice, she did her best to contain the emotions it brought to the surface. She missed him —terribly.

They discussed current builds, new builds, and a design change to the one in Saint Louis. They laughed about the bad Chinese food brought to the site and how the foreman ate six chocolate doughnuts each morning.

When business was over, Zach stood. "Well, Ed, we'll see you in a few days. But I'll let you talk to Darcy before you hang up."

He gave her a smile and then led Mary Ellen out of the room, and they shut the door behind them.

"I miss you." The words rushed out of her mouth.

"I miss you, too."

"I had coffee with Clara today at lunch. Just by chance. She walked into the Starbucks."

"You didn't spill anything on her, did you?"

They both laughed, but she leaned in to the speaker and whispered, "I know you have a tattoo."

"I sure do."

Okay, well, he wasn't hiding it. "I've never seen it."

"I keep my boxers on when you're around."

"I know. You're quite the gentleman." She looked around as if to check that they were alone. "I want to see it."

There was silence for a moment. "I'll show it to you." He was very matter-of-fact. "But it's not going to change anything."

She smiled, even alone in the room. "I wouldn't expect it to."

"You know, you're a part of that family."

"What do you mean?"

"I mean, in time, I want you to be."

She'd fought that damn lump in her throat and now tears stung her eyes. "You do?"

"I think you need a Keller tattoo. Besides, your family is just

239

as important. You'll always belong to your family, and well, you'll always belong in mine."

That was it. The first tear ran down her cheek, and she brushed it away quickly. "When you get home, we may have to look into that."

He agreed and they ended their phone call, but Darcy sat alone in the conference room and collected herself.

Ed Keller wanted her forever. She was ready.

CHAPTER 38

*T*he phone call that had come in on the morning Ed was expected home had completely ruined Darcy's mood.

It would be another four days before she saw him, and she didn't like the arrangement.

"I'll be home soon," he assured her.

"I don't mean to be so silly about it, but…"

"It's okay, Darcy. Trust me, I don't want to be here either." He let out a long breath. "My mom called and wants to have you over for dinner. She wasn't sure if you'd accept."

"Of course I'd accept."

"I told her as much. So Christian is expecting you to give him a ride over tonight."

Darcy laughed. "My mother and father used to do this. You know, she'd wonder what he was thinking, so she'd ask me and I'd find out."

"It's much the same in our family, only there are many more of us."

"It's a good thing I'm not shy."

"You can't be in this family." There was a brief silence before

Ed spoke again. "You haven't given any more thought about finding your birth parents, have you?"

"No." She was quick to answer. "I am who I am, and without my mom and dad, I wouldn't be me. Besides, what's to find? My dad told me that my birth mom died. Case closed."

"You didn't mention that before."

Darcy tapped her fingers on her desk. "It's not important anymore. It was what brought me to Nashville, and the rest has been fate."

"Well, if you ever change your mind…"

"I won't, but thank you."

"Enjoy your evening with my family."

Oh, she missed him something terrible. If she were more impulsive, she'd fly to Miami and meet him, but she wasn't like that. "I'll see you in a few days."

Ed had hated to deceive Darcy like he had, but it was all going to be worth the element of surprise. Now he sat in the showroom of an exclusive jewelry designer that his aunt Simone had set him up with in Miami.

He was about to make the biggest purchase of his life. Tomorrow he'd drive to her father's and ask for her hand in marriage.

Ed rubbed his palms together. He'd never been so nervous in all his life. This was crazy.

He'd negotiated multi-million dollar deals and met some of the world's most influential people, but looking now at the platinum ring setting and the two carat diamond that the jeweler placed in it to show him, he pegged himself for the next heart attack victim at Miami General.

The next morning, he called to make sure Christian was well taken care of before his surgery.

"It's no wonder Mom tried to have surgery without telling

anyone. She spent the night on my couch." He scoffed, and Ed laughed. "This isn't the first time I've gone through this."

"Yes, but you're still her baby boy."

"Right. So when are you coming home?"

"Tomorrow. I have some things I need to take care of first."

"Your girl is a little mopey without you. You'd better hurry home."

"Can you keep a secret? I'm going to plan a surprise party for her birthday."

"And you think this group can keep a secret?" Christian laughed.

"I think I'll just tell you and mom. That way everyone can show up for a dinner, and we'll have a party instead."

"Oh, so dinner on a Tuesday instead of a Sunday? Yep, she'll never see it coming."

"You are a smart-ass."

"And to think I used to be the quiet one."

That had Ed laughing. Baseball and locker rooms had completely transformed his brother from a shy boy to, well, a smart-ass. But still, there was no man who was more compassionate that Christian Keller. The woman who finally landed him for a husband would be well taken care of.

Ed disconnected the phone call with his brother and headed down the highway. Her father had moved to a small retirement community outside of Miami.

It was a nice setting, he thought, when he pulled through the front gate.

Each house looked exactly the same. Older men drove golf carts on the streets, and he'd seen more than one porch with a group of women sitting back and chatting.

Finally, he pulled up to the house that George McCary had given him the address to. An Marine flag waved in the breeze from the front porch. Yep, this was the place.

Before he could make it all the way to the door, a tall, strong man walked out of the front door and stood on the porch. His hair was cut high and tight, and he stood with his feet apart and his hands grasped behind his back. There was no mistaking this was Dr. George McCary, retired Marine.

Ed's mouth went dry, and he could feel the small, square box in his pocket digging uncomfortably into his upper thigh as he walked toward the man. Again, they might have to call for that ambulance that was going to carry him away. He'd simply never been so nervous.

"Mr. McCary?"

"Yup. You Eduardo Keller?"

"I am, sir." He held out his hand to the man. "It's a pleasure to meet you."

George McCary shook it firmly. The man might be working his way into his seventies, but Ed was very sure George McCary could easily kill him with one quick move.

"So, you're the man keeping my daughter in Nashville, huh?"

Ed swallowed hard. "That's what I'd like to discuss with you, sir."

George ran his tongue over his teeth. "Well, c'mon out back. My sister made some lemonade and set up the patio. She likes to fuss about like that."

George led him through the small house. Everything was tidy and clean, he noticed. Just as a military man would keep it. He thought of Darcy's small, dark apartment. The furniture wasn't hers and the space was very small, but she kept it neat as a pin. Now he knew why.

The patio on the back of the house faced many others like it. It was as if each neighborhood had a cul-de-sac of backyards instead of driveways.

Ed sat in the chair George pointed to. The ring box dug deeper into his leg.

George poured Ed a glass of lemonade and handed it to him. Then he did the same for himself and eased back in his chair.

"Well, Ed, let's cut to the chase. Something tells me you're not just dropping by for lemonade."

Ed cleared his through. "No, sir, I made a special trip to come see you."

"That would explain why you're alone, and Darcy never mentioned you coming by."

Ed nodded. "I've come seeking your blessing. I'd like to ask your daughter to marry me."

He'd done better than he thought he would. His voice hadn't wavered. But as he lifted his glass to his lips to ease the dryness that was nearly disabling him, he noticed his hands shook.

He quickly took the drink and lowered the glass.

George McCary wasn't a man to show emotion.

Ed thought better of it. Perhaps he knew how to show emotion—when he found the need to kill someone. Ed wasn't feeling threatened, so he took that as a good sign. But as the moments turned into minutes of silence, Ed thought maybe he'd rather have been run off the property.

"You haven't known Darcy very long."

"No, sir, I haven't."

"And you think you love her enough to want to marry her?"

"I know I do."

George gave a long, slow nod. "You're a successful man?"

"I'd like to think I am. I'm the vice president of Benson, Benson, and Hart."

"Nephew to the owner, I think she said."

"Yes." Ed hoped this man understood that nepotism wasn't a cushy job.

George McCary crossed his ankle over his knee and relaxed his shoulders. "My daddy owned a grocery store in Georgia when I was little. My friends always teased me about being rich because I got to work. Damned fools. They didn't know that working for your father's business means you have to start at the bottom and you don't usually get to the top."

Ed smiled. He did understand. "I started my job at fifteen on a job site. I have emptied my share of trash cans."

That made George laugh. They were making progress.

"She's a strong girl, my Darcy Ann."

"Yes, she is."

George rubbed the whiskers on his chin. "Is she still mad at us over the adoption thing?"

Ed bit down on his lip. "No, sir, I think she's over that. I told her I'd be happy to help her find her birth parents, if that would make her feel at ease, but she says she's not interested."

George nodded again, slowly. "I told her all I knew when she came to get me out of the hospital. She was born early because there was some kind of accident. She was six weeks early. Had a hard go of it there for a spell." He pursed his lips. "They told us the mom died." He shrugged. "I don't know anything about the daddy."

"I think that put her at ease."

"Good." George sat up straight in his chair and set his feet on the ground. "So, you want to ask her to marry you?"

"Yes." Ed reached into his pocket and pulled out the box that had been making him uncomfortable for more than one reason. "I've had this made for her."

He handed the small box to George, who opened it slowly. "Lord, have mercy."

Ed watched as George moved the box around so the ring would catch the light, but he never touched it, as if it might burn him.

"You had this made for my Darcy Ann?"

"Yes, sir."

"She's sure going to like it."

Those few words put a peace into Ed's chest that he hadn't felt in days. "I hope she will."

George closed the lid and handed it back to Ed. "She says you come from a big family. A good family."

Pride swelled in Ed's chest. "We are a very tight-knit group."

"From what she's told me, ya'll have taken really good care of her."

"My family loves her, sir."

George McCary gave Ed another long nod of consideration. "She loves you."

"I know she does, sir."

"You'll take care of her? She has a temper, and if she hasn't shown it to you yet, she will."

Ed laughed. "I won't run from it."

"She's always thought a lot about having a family."

"I welcome that."

"She's all I have in the world," he said, and his voice had softened.

"Mr. McCary, I love her. I will never let anything, or anyone, hurt her."

George McCary leaned in and rested his arms on his knees. "I believe you will take good care of my little girl." A smile formed on the corner of his mouth. "I give you my blessing."

CHAPTER 39

*D*arcy filled the ice bag again. It was a wonder people had children. One injured grown man was enough work for three grown women.

Since Christian had been released from the hospital he had done nothing but whine about the pain. It must have been the medication that made him so annoying. Darcy was sure he couldn't feel any pain, but he complained anyway.

His mother had run to the store to buy him something that he could keep down. There was nothing pretty about seeing a grown man get sick to his stomach.

Clara had tried to help out, but he'd gotten on her last nerve rather quickly. She'd bolted out the front door, and Darcy was fairly sure she'd flipped him the bird when she'd done so, though she'd never have done it so that her mother could see it.

Madeline opened the back door quietly and stepped in. "Is he still awake?"

"He was five minutes ago, but I haven't heard any groaning."

Madeline smiled. "He can deal with the surgery. It's always the pain meds that get him. And when he comes down off of them, he'll be sappy and apologetic."

"Really?" Darcy tightened the cap on the blue ice bag. "How many times has he had this surgery?"

"This is his second knee surgery. He had the other knee done a few years ago. There have been plenty of stitches and a broken wrist. That one was the worst. I suppose he'd have already made it to the major leagues if he hadn't had so many injuries."

Darcy looked out into the living room. It appeared Christian was sleeping peacefully. "Does it bother him to not be in the major leagues?"

Madeline shrugged. "He'd never say so, to me anyway. But I think that's every player's dream. Christian, however, will make one amazing coach someday. I think that will be his finest hour."

What a beautiful thing to say about your child, Darcy thought. Her mother always told her she'd have a house full of little boys. Why boys, she wasn't sure, but being around the Kellers and the absolute number of them, she was sure her mother was right. It seemed just the thing she would want to do—have a house full sons—in a few years.

"His follow-up appointment is Tuesday," Madeline mentioned as she put away the few items she'd purchased at the grocery store. "I make a mean chocolate cake, and I do believe I have boxes of unused candles, if I can convince you to have dinner with us on Tuesday after his appointment."

Darcy turned and could only smile. A moment later, when the emotions of the invitation settled, she was able to say, "I can't think of a better way to celebrate my twenty-fifth birthday."

Madeline gave her a nod and went out to check on Christian.

MADELINE HAD BEEN RIGHT. THE MOMENT CHRISTIAN'S medication wore off, he was all kinds of apologetic and sappy. He hugged his mother, and Darcy was sure he cried. Then when Madeline left him in Darcy's care, he did cry.

"I'm so mean when they give me those drugs. I'll bet I was horrible to you."

"You were fine. You seem to be getting back to yourself rather quickly."

He adjusted on the couch. "Sure. I'm great at this crash and burn stuff. This sucks." Now anger teetered in his voice. "I want to play damn ball. I don't want to keep being laid up like this."

"You'll recover very soon. Doesn't the team do physical therapy for you?"

That made him smile. "You know who is my therapist?" his words still slurred. "Tori."

"Tori?"

"Yeah, you met her at the fundraiser." The anger had certainly drained from his face. "I think we have a future."

Darcy laughed. "Does she know this?"

He shrugged. "We've gone out a few times. She's the sister-in-law to the pitcher. He says she likes me, but I'm a slow and easy kind of guy. No need to hurry things."

Darcy thought of Ed and how that statement didn't carry over to him. If he knew what he wanted, he went after it. Darcy was just lucky enough to be the one thing Eduardo Keller seemed to want.

It was nearly seven o'clock when the front door opened. Darcy jumped awake in her chair. She hadn't realized she'd fallen asleep sitting there talking to Christian, who didn't seem to be lying on the couch anymore.

Ed walked across the room and straight to her, pulling her out of the chair and taking possession of her mouth. It must have sparked the right amount electricity in her, and every one of her senses awakened.

She wrapped her arms around his neck and let him deepen the kiss. Oh, she'd missed him.

He didn't pull away, but he rested his head against hers. "I think it would be a good idea to take my assistant with me on every trip from now on."

"Your assistant thinks that would be a very good idea."

"Your brother thinks it sucks. She's a great nurse." Christian's voice came from the other room, and they both turned to see him rested on his crutches in the doorway. "But she took such good care of me that you two should head out of here and leave me alone."

A smile formed on Ed's lips. "And I'm just unsentimental enough to take you up on that and make you fend for yourself."

"Ed," Darcy whispered against his chest.

"Okay, okay. He's lucky you only live downstairs, but I'm taking her downstairs."

"Be gone with you." Christian motioned for them to walk past.

Darcy stopped as she got to the door. "Yell if you need me. The doors are open into the house. I can be up in just a moment."

"I'll be fine," Christian said.

Ed gave her hand a squeeze. "I'll be down in just a moment."

Darcy gave him a nod and descended the stairs.

CHAPTER 40

*W*hen she was clearly out of ear shot, Ed turned back to Christian.

"Mom said she invited Darcy to dinner Tuesday."

Christian nodded. "Promised to make her a chocolate cake and fill it with candles."

Ed smiled. "Good. I'll take you to your appointment and then we'll head over. It will be totally unassuming."

Christian adjusted the crutch under his arm. "You're really going to do this?"

Ed looked around to make sure Darcy wasn't headed back up the steps. He reached into his pocket and pulled out the box he carried. He opened it, and Christian's eyes went wide.

"Holy cow!" He looked closer. "You're serious."

"I don't mess around with this stuff. You know that."

Christian nodded. "She's going to love that."

"I got her father's blessing, too. Scariest thing I've ever done in my life."

Christian laughed. "I'm happy for you. I really am."

"Good, and you'll stand up with me when we get married?"

The smile on Christian's face grew wider. "I would never want to be anywhere else."

Ed handed him the box. "Hold on to this. Your job is to get it to me on Tuesday at dinner."

"You got it."

Ed gave him a pat on the shoulder and hurried off to be with Darcy.

He could hear her in the bathroom. She was washing her face.

They'd spent enough nights together that he knew her routine before bed, her breathing pattern when she slept, and just how beautiful she was when she woke with the promise of a new day.

This would be forever—soon. This woman, whom he'd only met less than two months ago, was his dream come true. His forever.

Until she'd taken his face in her hands and kissed him that night he stood her up, he didn't know it would come this far. But when you knew love was right there, you grabbed it with both hands and you held on tight.

Darcy walked out of the bathroom, turned off the light, and jumped when she saw him standing there. "I didn't know you were down here."

"I was just waiting for you to come out."

She smiled sweetly and moved closer to him. She was already in her pajamas which, though pinstriped and too big, were very sexy.

"It's not even eight o'clock. Are you heading to bed?"

"Not unless you have other thoughts on our sleeping arrangements." She playfully lifted her brows.

Ed reached his fingers into her hair. "Oh, I have plenty of ideas."

He pulled her into to him and quickly took possession of her mouth. The fresh taste of mint against his tongue sent a surge through him. There was no way, feeling as he did at that moment, he'd make it until they were married. Not that he'd truly intended on not sleeping with the woman he loved, but he was trying to be a gentleman. However, his body was quickly taking over his manners.

He moved his hands to the buttons on her pajama top. The moan that came from her throat told him she was on the same page with her emotions, too.

Darcy's hands went straight for his belt.

There was no turning back now. He almost wished he'd kept the ring in his pocket. Wouldn't that have surprised her? But that wasn't the plan. Oh, hell, his head was swimming with her in his hands, what did he care about plans?

As Darcy pulled his belt from the loops on his pants, she broke the kiss.

Her chest, bare under her pajamas and now playing peek-a-boo with the fabric, heaved.

"I want to see that tattoo." The smile that turned up the corner of her mouth was nearly pure devil. He liked it.

Ed unbuttoned his pants and quickly pushed them to the floor. He stood, very exposed, in his boxers.

Darcy bit her lip and looked down. There was no denying what part of his body was working the hardest.

"You'll find it just under the band," he suggested, trying to keep his voice solid.

Darcy gazed into his eyes. There was love there—so much love. And trust. She trusted him with everything. He could see that, as if he could see into her soul.

But he blinked and broke the gaze when her finger slipped under the band of his boxers.

This was it. Time's up.

Darcy shifted her eyes to where her hand folded down the band on fabric, which was not concealing much at the moment.

His entire body quaked as she ran her finger over the infinity symbol with the word family intertwined on it.

The smile she flashed him was different now. It smoldered, just as her eyes did.

She held up her left wrist. "I want mine here."

"Done." He sucked in a breath. "Tomorrow seems like a great day to do that."

She nodded and moved her mouth back to his.

But the moment was gone when they heard an enormous crash from upstairs and a slew of curses from Christian.

The smoldering looks were now filled with fear and panic.

Ed reached for his pants and somehow managed to get them on as he ran up the stairs.

Darcy was right behind him.

As they ran from the kitchen and into the living room, they saw the mess they had heard.

Christian sat on the floor, next to the overturned coffee table. His hand was on his forehead, and blood dripped from under it.

"Crap! What did you do?" Ed ran to his brother as Darcy ran to the kitchen for a towel.

"I guess I'm a little dizzy. I went to stand up and fell over."

Darcy handed Ed the towel, and Christian grinned. "Nice top, Darcy."

Ed turned and noticed it was still hanging open, but she was frantically buttoning it. He smacked Christian in the arm.

"What's that for?"

"You're a pig," Ed said as he examined the cut over his brother's brow. "You're going to need stitches."

"Damn it!"

"Don't be such a baby."

"You know if you were in my shoes, you'd be crying."

Ed shook his head as he held the towel to his brother's head. "I'm pretty sure I've always been stronger emotionally."

The conversation stopped there.

Ed stood and motioned to Darcy to grab Christian's crutches. Then he pulled him to his feet.

"C'mon. When was the last time you were in the clinic?"

"Seriously? You're taking me there?"

"Curtis is working tonight. He'll love stabbing you with a needle."

Ed made sure Christian was stable and the bleeding had stopped enough before he turned to Darcy.

"I'll be back."

"Don't you want me to go with you?"

Ed touched her face. "You get some rest. And tomorrow, we'll go get that tattoo."

She smiled, but she wasn't happy about any of it. Those damn beautiful brown eyes sure could tell him a lot about this woman. And yet, deep down, they held some kind of secret he didn't know about. He wasn't sure she did either. Darcy McCary, the future Mrs. Eduardo Keller, was so familiar to him, which was the rush to make her all his. But those eyes...what were they hiding?

CHAPTER 41

*E*d wondered how it was that late on a Friday night a medical clinic could be so busy. He and Christian had been waiting almost an hour, and dropping the name Curtis Keller had done nothing to get them in any faster.

It was nearing ten o'clock when they were finally called back.

A nurse took Christian's vitals and flashed a smile at him when he turned on his charm.

Ed shook his head. Where had this man come from? Christian had been such a shy kid, emotional, and, well, a total nerd. The minute he made his first varsity baseball team, a new man emerged and he had a healthy dose of smart ass to add to the mix that made Christian Keller.

Curtis pulled back the curtain and laughed. "I promised I'd be at dinner on Tuesday. You don't have to keep showing up."

"Funny," Christian scoffed. "Just fix this please."

Curtis took a look at the cut on his head. "You're just an accident waiting to happen, aren't you?"

"Waiting? Look at me. I'm messed up from head to toe."

"You're going to need about four stitches."

"Really?" Christian's shoulders dropped. "Women dig scars, right?"

"So they tell me." Curtis poked at the wound with a gloved hand, and Christian winced.

Ed could feel his airport dinner churning in his stomach.

"Let me get the stuff I need to fix this up."

Curtis left the curtained-off area.

"This isn't how I wanted to spend my weekend," Christian complained.

"You're tough." Ed looked at his watch. "Hey, is that tattoo parlor still open where we got our family tattoos?"

Christian shrugged. "I think so. Why? You getting Darcy's name tattooed on your butt?"

Ed laughed. "It's a thought. No. She's going to get the family tattoo on her wrist, like Clara's."

Christian narrowed his eyes. "I can't believe you're this serious about her."

"You think I'm wrong about her."

"No. Oh, no," he was quick to answer. "I like her. I like her a lot. In fact, had you not gotten to her first, well…"

Ed didn't want to think about that more than he already had.

Christian adjusted on the bed. "I've just never seen you so… possessive over someone."

"Possessive?"

"It's like you were meant to take care of her. I don't know." He touched his head. "I'm still fuzzy."

Curtis returned with a metal tray full of utensils and went about stitching up Christian's head.

Ed sunk into his hard, plastic chair and diverted his eyes. He didn't want to see what was going on in front of him.

But Christian's words kept playing in his head. It's like you were meant to take care of her.

He was right. That was exactly what it was like. She was a gift. She fell right into his life. God, he was a lucky man.

Curtis finished stitching up Christian's head. "Keep it dry until tomorrow. I'll go get you ointment to put on it to keep it sanitary."

Curtis left again, and Christian sat up on the bed. "I was thinking, did Darcy ever find anything on her birth parents?"

"No." He didn't want to tell him about her searching the company records. It didn't sound too good. "She gave up the search. She decided it wasn't too important. Besides, when she went to see her dad, he told her that her birth mother had died."

"That's sad."

"She's fine."

"But if her birth mother died then, really, there's no harm in finding out who she was right?"

"Why?"

"To know."

Ed shook his head. "I told her I'd help her find them if she wanted, but she said she's fine. So that's that."

Christian nodded, but he was still thinking.

Curtis came back into the curtained area with a tube and handed it to Christian. "Here. Use this to keep it moist."

Christian nodded, exchanged a glance with Ed, and then looked back at Curtis. "If someone was born in the hospital, could you look up their records?"

Ed pursed his lips, but Christian just narrowed his eyes.

"Depends. You got a kid you didn't know about?"

Christian laughed. "Not that I know. How far back can you go?"

"If it's further than ten years, we have to order up charts. What's this about?"

Ed didn't like this, but there was something about wanting to know himself that kept him from stopping Christian.

"Darcy came to Nashville to find her birth parents. She was born in Nashville General. What can you do?"

Curtis shrugged. "I could look her up. What's her full name and birthdate?"

Ed winced before he spoke. "Darcy Ann McCary."

"And her parents were here when she was born? They are the ones on her birth certificate?"

"Yes."

Curtis reached into the pocket of his jacket and took out a note pad. He wrote down her name. "What are her parents' names?"

"George and Francis McCary."

Curtis nodded. "What date?"

"August twenty-first. Twenty-five years ago."

Curtis stopped writing. "Really?"

"Yeah, why?"

He shook his head. "No reason." He tucked the note pad back into his coat. "I can't even start to get this processed until Monday. And my ass is on the line if I give you the info. So as far as you know, you don't know. Got it?"

Both Ed and Christian nodded.

"But if the mother died in child birth then I don't really see a problem. You might have the information by Tuesday, if you were looking at giving it to her for her birthday."

Christian grinned. "Yep. I thought that would be the perfect present."

Ed wasn't so sure.

CHAPTER 42

*D*arcy had been asleep when Ed had crawled into bed with her. She was so comfortable with him around her that it never fazed her when she heard him come in.

This would be what it was like, she thought as morning broke and the deep breaths of the man she loved were the only sounds. It would be them, in their bed, waking as man and wife. She wondered when he would actually ask her to marry him. He'd hinted to it enough. There was time, she reminded herself as she moved closer into Ed's sleeping embrace.

By ten o'clock, Ed had finally stumbled out of the bedroom. He raked his fingers through his thick hair.

"What are you doing?" he asked as he looked down at Darcy, who was now sitting on the floor surrounded by boxes.

"I'm going through all the stuff my father sent me home with. My mother saved all of this for me, and now I have to decide what to do with it."

"What is it?"

"I would assume this is my hope chest."

Ed rubbed the back of his neck. "As in someday you hope to get married and here are things for your house?"

"Yep. There are tea-towels that my grandmother, whom I never met, cross-stitched. Some silver spoons. No forks, just silver spoons. Linens, table cloths, and a box of mismatched china plates."

Ed nodded. "Can't beat eclectic."

Darcy laughed. Eclectic. That word seemed to sum up her life. Not only had her past been an eclectic tide of military-base houses, schools and friends, but now she was becoming part of a family, which in its own right was eclectic.

When she thought about his family, she thought about the tattoo they were going to get for her.

"Do you think that tattoo place is open now?"

Ed shrugged. "I don't know. But how about I run home, get a shower and some clean clothes, and I'll pick you up for lunch and we can go after."

Darcy smiled. "Sounds like a plan."

THREE HOURS LATER, DARCY WAS HAVING SECOND THOUGHTS. SHE was seated in the tattoo parlor with her arm stretched out. They had already drawn the outline that the man, bald and tattooed on every part of his body, had put down. Ed held tight to her other hand as the whir of the tattoo pen started.

The moment the pen touched her arm, she gritted her teeth and gripped tighter to Ed's hand. She'd never felt such pain. Tears welled in her eyes, and she squeezed them shut. This pain would be over soon, but the precious meaning behind the tattoo would last forever.

"You're doing great," Ed said as the word family was formed on her arm.

"Why do people do this?" she whispered as she winced.

"To make it forever."

His voice was soft over the whir of the pen, and suddenly, it didn't hurt anymore. The pain was nothing in comparison to the meaning.

It seemed like it had been hours, but in no time, she was marked for life. The dark ink against the red swollen skin was the most beautiful thing she'd ever seen.

"I can't believe I did that. My mother is probably giving God an earful right now."

Ed laughed. "I think it looks wonderful. I can't wait for my mother to see it."

"Why?"

"This design was all her idea. Just like shaving our heads, I don't think she thought we'd all follow suit."

Darcy held her arm, as if she'd smudge the art work under the loose piece of gauze, as they left the parlor. She looked at him. "What did you mean you shaved your head?"

Ed opened the door to his truck and helped her in. Then he walked around to the other side before he answered. "When Mom started losing her hair, my dad shaved it off. Then he told her to shave his. She wouldn't do it. So he took the clippers down the center of his head."

Darcy laughed out loud. "He did not."

"Yep. Then he told her she had to finish it."

"Oh," the tears began to fall, "that is beautiful."

Ed started the truck and pulled out of the lot. "We all got home as they were in the bathroom laughing. So I sat down and made her shave my head."

Darcy reached over and placed her hand on his arm. "That is precious."

"Well, Clara and Christian chickened out."

She laughed. "Christian did? I wouldn't think that was his style."

"Back then it was." He turned the corner. "Anyway, it was when Dad was engaged to Kathy. She was not impressed, but I'm glad he did it. It meant the world to Mom."

"And that was why you all got that tattoo?"

Ed smiled. "Yeah. She said she was going to do it, and we all showed up. She cried the whole time."

"I assume not just because it hurt."

He only smiled, but she understood it.

CHAPTER 43

*E*d couldn't wait for his mother to see what Darcy had done, so he drove to his parents' house. His father was mowing the lawn, which reminded Ed that he'd better do the same. If his grandfather ever saw the yard in its current state, he'd take back the house.

His mother was on her knees digging in the flower bed that the family had spent a weekend building for her a few years ago. It seemed when her children moved away, she still had the need to grow things and watch them blossom.

His father turned off the mower as they climbed out of the truck. "Well, look who came to finish the lawn."

Ed laughed. "That didn't work when I lived here."

"Don't I know it." He shook his hand. "Hello, Darcy," he said and leaned in to give her a kiss on the cheek.

Ed smiled. She'd become accustom to it in time, the affection his entire family would shower on her. A powerful feeling rose in him. He couldn't wait to see the expression on everyone's faces when he proposed on Tuesday. Darcy thought the tattoo was overwhelming, emotionally. He was going to knock her socks off.

His mother stood from her kneeling pad and pulled off her

gardening gloves. "What a nice surprise." She kissed Ed on the cheek and then did the same to Darcy. "What brings you two by?"

Ed nudged Darcy. "Show her."

Darcy lifted the tape from her skin and pulled back the gauze cover to reveal her new tattoo.

Just as Ed had expected, his mother's eyes filled with tears.

"Oh, Darcy, it's beautiful," she said as she raised her hand to her chest. "Carlos, look."

"That's some mighty nice ink," he complimented as he rested a hand on Ed's shoulder.

"I hope you don't mind that I used your design. Ed suggested it, and it's just such a beautiful design."

"Oh, why would I ever mind?" His mother wiped away her tear. "My son loves you, and you're part of this family as well as your own. I'm honored."

She pulled Darcy into a hug—not just any hug—but one that crushed your bones and filled your heart with love. Yep, this was the right woman. If he loved her as much as he did, and his family loved her too, how could it be wrong?

DARCY LAY IN ED'S BED, WRAPPED IN HIS ARMS. AFTER THEY'D visited his parents, he seemed to be very conscious of the fact he hadn't been home much. So very domestically, they'd gone back to his place and she had vacuumed and dusted while he had mowed the lawn. Darcy had never been more comfortable.

She lifted her arm to look at the tattoo on her wrist in the moonlit shadows of Ed's room. Family. Never in all her life did she think she'd mark her body so permanently, but it meant everything to her.

Ed caressed her shoulder and then placed a kiss against her skin. "Does it hurt?"

"It itches, but it's just so beautiful."

"You're beautiful."

She giggled. But then a serious thought filled her head, and the need for an answer squeezed at her heart. "You love me, right?"

"Yes."

"And you said I'm part of this family."

"Yes," he said, but his voice waivered. "What are you getting at?"

Darcy turned to face him. "I love you. I'm just so glad that I bumped into you that day."

Ed smiled. "I'm glad you say that. You were pretty pissed."

"No. I was embarrassed. Besides, my mind was focused on something so unimportant now." How could she ever have wanted to chase down who she was? She knew who she was. But she pushed that thought out of her head. "Is this forever? Tell me, do you really want me forever?"

Ed propped himself up on his elbow. "Yes. Are you doubting me?"

"No. I'm—oh, I don't know. It all seems so fast."

"And time means nothing when you fall in love, and neither does age."

Darcy nodded. "You do want to marry me, right?"

The worry in his eyes softened. "Yes. When the time is right, I want to marry you."

"And family?"

"The bigger, the better—unless you don't want kids." The line between his brows deepened.

"Oh, no. I want kids. And having been alone all my life and now seeing what you have, I want lots of kids."

"That's a relief."

"But I don't know anything about who they'll be."

Ed ran his fingers down her arm. "They'll be you and me."

"I understand that. But I don't know if I have some strange genes that, well, maybe they won't be perfect."

Ed shook his head. "A child is perfect." He sat up, and she

followed. Ed turned so he was fully facing her as if he had a point to make. "Darcy, I have every intention of marrying you and having a family with you. I don't care who you were before you were a McCary. And I'm not much different in not knowing what will come from me when we have kids. My dad knows almost nothing about his own genes, but we all turned out okay. Besides, even if there is something quirky that happens, I'm going to love any child you give me."

The ache in her chest eased. "You're going to marry me?"

He smiled again. "I'm going to marry you, and don't you dare think this is your proposal. I'm going to make that special."

"I can't imagine you could top the feeling I have right now."

He caressed her cheek. "I promise."

Darcy took his hands in hers and then shifted her eyes to his. "Are you really going to make me wait until our wedding night to make love to you?"

Ed's mouth curled into that sexy smile she loved. "I take it you're over my being a gentleman."

"I'm so over it."

"And being totally modern, the whole premarital sex thing is okay with you"

She bit down on her lip. "Ed, I told you, I'm not a virgin. I don't know where you decided I needed to be handled so gently."

"I'm just clarifying…because I'm over it, too."

And with that, his hands came to her hair, and he pulled her to him. His mouth was hot and more eager than she'd ever known. This wasn't a mistake. This was true love, and as he lowered her back to the bed and moved on top of her, she tumbled into the abyss of absolute happiness.

CHAPTER 44

*D*arcy finished her work on Tuesday afternoon and turned off her computer. She wondered if she'd truly accomplished anything. Her head had been in the clouds for the past few days.

Ed had turned her world upside down when she met him, but when he made love to her—time stood still.

In time, perhaps, it would be the normal to be so happy. But, for now, she was enjoying the euphoria of happiness.

Darcy looked around and wondered how she was going to get home with all of the office gifts she'd received for her birthday. Mary Ellen had ordered a birthday cake, which they had cut at lunch. She'd brought her a birthday basket full of bath salts and lotions, too. The human resource department had sent her flowers, and one of the ladies from accounting had brought her balloons. She'd never had this much attention on her birthday. How could anyone top it?

Ed called her from his office, and she turned and walked through the door, an enormous smile pushing at her cheeks.

"You look happy," he said.

"I'm in awe of all the attention I've been given today. Top that with the fact that I'm absolutely in love with the greatest man in the world, and yeah—I'm happy."

"Is this guy you love as good looking as me?" He gave her a wink. "Okay, I'm headed out to pick up Christian and take him to his appointment. Mom is expecting you whenever you get done here. She's worried you won't like lasagna."

"I love lasagna."

"Good answer." He smiled as he picked up his keys. "I love you. I'll see you soon." He walked around his desk and pressed a long, hard kiss to her lips and then turned to walk out the door. "By the way," he said as he walked away, "you're not going to be living in the basement much longer. I think you'd better start packing and just move in with me."

He never looked back. He just kept walking.

Darcy's heart beat faster in her chest. She looked down at her wrist, and the tattoo that she'd branded herself with. She squeezed her eyes closed. Family—and Ed was hers.

CHRISTIAN HOBBLED TO THE TRUCK, AND ED TAPPED HIS FINGERS on his arms, which were folded. "You are so slow."

"Next week, I'll kick your ass for that."

"I bet you will," Ed laughed as he watched his brother struggle to climb into the truck. He'd help him if he needed it, but he was sure Christian would do anything just to be a little independent.

Once he was in, Ed closed the door and walked around to the other side. He climbed in and started the truck.

"Oh, before I forget," Christian said as he dug into his pocket and pulled out the ring box, "I don't want to be responsible for this anymore."

Ed opened the box and looked down at the ring. It was perfect. Darcy had been happy when he'd left her at the office, but in a few hours, she'd be over the moon.

"So you're going to ask her tonight?" Christian asked as he fastened his seat belt.

"Yep. Or at least make it official. We've been doing a lot of talking about it."

"I'm happy for you. I was beginning to wonder if your time had run out." He laughed.

Ed had, at times, wondered that too.

Ed pulled up in front of the hospital and let Christian out, and then went to park. As he climbed out of the truck, he received the text message from Darcy that she was at his parents' house with his aunts, cooking dinner.

He could only imagine the chaos in the kitchen, the laughing, and the gossip.

Ed walked through the hospital, and the thought that his future wife had made her entrance into the world in that very building on that very day was a bit surreal. How amazing that her path in life would bring her back to Nashville and to him.

Christian was already in the exam room when Ed made it to him.

"Do they need to cut your leg off, or do you get to keep it?"

"Totally get to keep it, but we are discussing bionic upgrades." Christian laughed. "Oh, and if you want to get going, you can. Uncle Curtis is on his way over from the clinic. They found Darcy's records. He's on his way to pick them up."

A chill ran down Ed's spine. He still wasn't sure he liked the idea of giving her the information, but what would it hurt? The woman who had given Darcy away was dead, and soon, she'd be his wife—he'd always take care of her.

Ed looked at his watch. It really wouldn't be anything to wait for his brother and uncle, but it would be a few more minutes with his love if he could ditch his brother.

"So he'll bring you to dinner then?"

"He said he's headed that way after he's done here. I'll catch a ride with him."

Ed nodded and turned for the door.

"Hey, Ed," Christian called, and he turned back. "I'm really excited for you. I can't wait to see the expression on her face when you give her the ring. So make sure I'm there."

"I will."

THE FRAGRANT AROMA OF GARLIC FROM HIS MOTHER'S HOUSE MET Ed out in street. She was putting on a spread.

It wasn't that he was late, but this family loved a dinner together, which was why they did it so often. His sister's car was already there. Regan, Zach, John, and Arianna were there. Tyler's car was there which meant Spencer was there too. Avery must have come with her mother, for they traveled as a pair most the time. And, of course, Darcy's monster of a truck was parked there, too.

Ed let out a breath. He was going to have a big audience tonight.

When he walked through the front door of the house, it was no surprise that his grandparents sat on the couch. He walked right to them and kissed them both before finding his mother in the kitchen.

"Oh good, you're here," she said as she stirred the sauce on the stove. "Find your father and help him set up that extra table."

Ed kissed his mother's cheek and walked out to the family room where they had set up the longer tables. Darcy stood with Tyler and Spencer, enjoying a laugh. When she looked up, they all turned his way.

Their eyes. What a strange thing to notice, all the sudden. They all had the same eyes.

Darcy walked across the room and placed a gentle kiss on his lips. "Hello, handsome."

"You sure do fit in here, don't you?"

"I do." She waved her wrist to acknowledge the tattoo. "Where is your brother?"

"He's coming with Curtis." He looked around the room, and he noticed everyone was watching him. So much for secrets.

Darcy laid her hands on his chest. "Are you alright?"

He smiled. "I'm absolutely perfect." And he was. Everyone he cared about was right there, staring at him. Well, almost everyone.

"What is that?" Darcy asked as she rested her hand on his chest pocket.

Ed felt the color drain from his face. He'd meant to put the ring in another pocket, but now she had her hand over it.

The smiles on the faces of his family told him he couldn't wait another second. Christian would have to forgive him.

"It's your birthday present."

Darcy licked her lips nervously and then looked around. "My...present?" She sucked in a breath.

Ed took her hands in his. "I didn't have a meeting in Florida."

"Then why did you go?"

"I went to meet your father."

"Oh," she choked out.

"I know we've talked about this, but sometimes things have to be done just right. So I went to Florida to meet your father and ask him for his blessing."

She batted her eyes quickly, and he could see them fill with tears.

Ed dropped to one knee, Darcy's hands still held in his. He could see his mother move to his father's side and wipe her eyes.

"Darcy, he gave me his blessing."

"Oh, God." Her hand shook in his, and the tears no longer restrained themselves to her eyes. They began to roll down her cheeks.

Ed smiled and pulled the box from his pocket as he heard the front door open and slam shut. Good, his brother wouldn't miss this.

From the corner of his eye he saw Curtis rush into the room, a manila envelope in his hands. But he stopped quickly when he saw what was going on.

The envelope moved from sight, and his uncle stepped back behind his aunt.

Ed opened the box, and Darcy gasped. He took the ring from the box and held it at the tip of her left ring finger. "Darcy McCary, will you marry me?"

The answer was almost muffled by her sobs and the sobs of all the others in the room. But she nodded quickly, giving him his answer.

Ed slid the ring on her finger, stood, and then gathered her in his arms as his family rushed in around them.

Everyone except Curtis and now Christian, who stood just beyond everyone with the most horrified looks on their faces.

Ed made sure to hug and kiss everyone, but he needed to get to those two. Something must have happened with Christian. His surgery must have...

No, there was something in that envelope that Curtis quickly made disappear when he'd walked in the room.

He smiled at his grandmother, who cupped his face in her hands. "She belongs here," she said.

Yes, she did.

CHAPTER 45

Curtis and Christian had kept their distance through dinner. But as Darcy blew out the candles on her cake, Ed finally moved toward them.

"Are you two okay? You seem very out of sorts for being at a party."

Curtis nodded. "Congratulations."

"Thank you." Ed turned to Christian. "Did everything go okay at your appointment? They don't really have to cut off your leg, do they?" He was trying to be humorous, but it wasn't working.

His family moved around the room, each with cake and a smile on their face. Ed couldn't figure out why these two were moping around.

"What's this?" Simone turned the corner with the manila envelope in her hand. She'd already pulled the contents out before Curtis made a lunge for her.

The room had gone silent. But the shock on her face said there was something there that they all needed to know.

Simone put the papers back into the envelope and quickly handed it back to Curtis.

Darcy moved to Ed's side.

Ed inched toward his uncle. "What's going on? Is that what I think it is? Are those Darcy's records?"

"Not now, Ed. Not here." Curtis tucked them under his arm.

"Wait, you found my birth record? You found my parents?" Darcy was now right next to him again.

Curtis took a step back. "I said not here. Not now."

"Something is wrong?" Darcy turned and set her cake on the counter and then turned back to Curtis. "Oh, God, what did you find?"

Curtis turned to leave with the envelope, but Christian pulled it from his hands.

"This is what he found." His voice had an evil tone that Ed had never heard before.

Curtis made a move to pull the papers away, but Ed held his hand up to ward him off. Whatever they found was going to affect him, or they wouldn't be acting this way.

Darcy was close enough that he could feel her breath on his arm. Someone else in the room moved quickly, as if they knew what was in the envelope.

Ed pulled out the papers and took a good, long look at the medical record from the night Darcy was born.

She was born premature.

She was in distress.

It had been a C-section birth.

The mother had been beaten and was in ICU.

Dr. Curtis Keller was present.

George and Francis McCary were there to take guardianship of the child.

And the baby's mother, Regan Keller, was not to have contact with the baby.

There was no describing the anger that burned in Ed's chest. He'd forgotten there was once mention of a baby. The thought never crossed his mind when Darcy happened into his life. But now, here she stood—and the information she'd been looking for was right in his hand.

He'd never felt so deceived.

He took a step to distance himself from her. "This is what you wanted? This is why you wanted to get close to me?"

Darcy's eyes opened wide. "What are you talking about? I love you."

"Do you? Or was it just part of your plan to get this information? You looked in our files. You infiltrated our family."

Tears were streaming from her eyes. "Ed, what does it say?"

Regan moved in behind her and held her hands out. "Give me the file."

"I want to hear it from Darcy. I want to know she used me."

Her lip quivered. "I don't know what you're talking about."

Regan ripped the papers out of his hand and looked down at them. "Oh, dear Lord." She covered her mouth as Zach moved to her side. "I never thought this would happen."

Darcy watched Regan and then turned back to Ed. "What's going on?"

"You make me sick. I can't believe I fell for your lies. You came here to find your birth mother. Did you ever think of what that would do to her or her family? There is a reason people don't tell their children they're adopted. Sometimes the truth is too terrible."

Darcy's eyes narrowed on him, and then they grew wide. She turned back to Regan, who sobbed next to her. "Oh. Oh! I didn't..."

"How can I trust you?"

"How can you not?" she argued. "I love you."

"You used me."

"Ed..."

"Get out of here. You don't really belong here at all."

. . .

Darcy took the ring off her finger and pressed it into Ed's hand, and then ran as fast as she could out of the house.

The truck took its time turning over, but finally, it roared to life and she sped away from the house.

Her vision blurred, and she fought to keep breath in her lungs. She had no idea. None. How could she have known she was the daughter of Regan Keller? There was no way she could have known.

She wiped at her eyes as she screeched to a stop at a stoplight. She had to get out of Nashville. She had to go home. Home. Home—which wasn't there anymore.

She wasn't even sure how she'd made it back to her apartment. The entire trip, the entire night, was just a blur.

Darcy threw the truck into park in the driveway and ran around the side of the house. The steps were steeper than she'd remembered, and she stepped off one and nearly slid down the concrete stairs.

Once she caught her breath, she shoved her key into the lock and jiggled it. She tried to calm herself down, tried to keep from shaking, but it was no use. She couldn't get the door open.

With tears streaking her face, she finally managed the lock and nearly fell inside when she twisted the door knob.

There was no time. She had to pack, and she had to do it quickly. If she never saw another Keller, it would be too soon. But that only made her cry more. She was a Keller. The forgotten Keller. The one the Kellers gave away.

There was a reason she felt so comfortable with those people. That was her family, and she'd been robbed of it.

She wiped her nose with the back of her hand. Ed was her damn cousin. Just as quickly, she realized they weren't related at all. His father was adopted. Her birth mother was adopted. There was no blood that was shared there.

They had been lovers. They had been in love. All of that was gone now. He hated her. They all hated her.

Darcy went straight to her bedroom and pulled her suitcase out from under her bed. She began to fill it with clothes from her closet and from the drawers of her dresser. It didn't matter how it landed. It just had to be done.

Then she moved to the bathroom, taking an empty box with her. She filled it with all the items in the drawers. Luckily she'd already repacked the boxes her mother had saved for her. After all, Ed had asked her to move in with him. God, how stupid could she have been?

It had been an hour since she'd hurried away from the Keller's house, and in that short time, her life was packed up and ready to go—well, she didn't know where. All she knew was that before anyone could get to her, she'd be gone.

Darcy picked up her suitcase and swung open the door. She nearly slammed the door again when she saw a woman standing in the now dark stairwell.

It was Regan.

CHAPTER 46

$\mathcal{D}$arcy's hand tightened around the handle of the suitcase. She didn't say a word. She didn't know what to say.

"Can I come in?" Regan asked in the same soft voice Darcy had always known her to have.

Her heart ached as she looked at the woman in a different light. This woman gave her life. This woman gave her away.

This woman was here now.

Darcy stepped back and let Regan into the apartment.

She looked around at the now packed up space. "You know, in all the years I lived upstairs, I never came down here when they turned it into an apartment. It's nice."

Darcy shut the door and set her suitcase down. The air was thick in her lungs. She had so many questions, but the words were not coming.

Regan turned to look at her. She clasped her hands in front of her. "Did you know it was me you were looking for?"

Darcy shook her head.

"I believe you."

"You believe me, but Ed doesn't?" Her voice was shaky and soft.

"He will when I'm done with him."

Regan stood there. She scanned a look over Darcy from head to toe, and then she smiled.

"I've always wondered what you looked like."

Darcy pursed her lips as if it would keep the tears at bay. "You did?"

Regan nodded. "I've never seen you before. When you were born, I closed my eyes. I didn't want to see you. I loved you too much. Only Curtis saw you."

Her words squeezed at her heart, and it hurt. She'd never hurt this bad. "Why wouldn't you want to see me? You gave me away."

Regan's shoulders rose and then dropped. "I did. I needed to." She looked around. "Can we sit? I really need to tell you all of this. I won't feel right if you leave and don't have the answers you came for. Besides, there hasn't been a day in twenty-five years I haven't thought about you. I'd like to have a few moments."

Darcy didn't know what to do with that. If she'd thought about her, why didn't she come for her?

Regan sat down on the couch, so Darcy took the chair.

Regan took a deep breath. "I don't even know where to begin." She looked down at her hands, which shook, and then up at Darcy and smiled. "First of all, you're beautiful. You're more beautiful than I ever could have imagined."

Darcy bit down on her lip. "Thank you."

"I'm glad I got to spend some time with you before all this. I enjoyed your company immensely. Ed is lucky to have you."

"I don't think he feels that way."

"We'll see. Don't give up on him yet." Regan adjusted on the couch. "His name was Michael Hamilton."

Darcy just looked at her and then eased back in her chair when she realized that was the name of her birth father. At that moment, she felt dizzy. This was really happening. She hadn't prepared herself for the moment when she would actually get the information she'd craved.

Regan wiped her brow with the back of her hand. "I killed him nineteen years ago."

Darcy reminded herself to breathe. That certainly wasn't what she'd expected. But then Ed's story, about the man Regan had once been involved with, entered her mind.

"In the theater?"

This time, Regan's eyes shot open wide. "Yes. How did you know that?"

"Ed said something about a man you'd been involved with before you met Zach. He told me the man had beaten you nearly to death and then came back. He said that you shot him."

Regan nodded. "I forget how much they know. I don't know if he ever knew about the baby—you."

"He beat you. My dad said I was born in trauma. He thought it was an accident. He said they were told my mother died, and that I was six weeks early and fought for my life."

Regan rubbed her hands together. This was obviously making her nervous, perhaps it even pained her.

Darcy was uncomfortable, and she genuinely felt sorry for Regan. But she had to know.

"We were engaged. I met him when I'd moved to L.A. and then we moved to Hawaii. I was so in love with him. He was rich and charismatic. I had the most enormous engagement ring and a beautiful wardrobe." She stopped for a moment to collect herself. "He was happy about you. Excited. We had a nursery, and he'd bought little outfits. But he was lying to me the whole time. One day he came home and he told me that he'd married someone else."

"Married someone else?"

Regan nodded. "Yes. She was a wealthy woman and that was very important to him. I was just the daughter of immigrants."

"That's terrible."

"He couldn't afford to have me—us—in his life. So he set out to kill me. And you."

The tears came then. Darcy couldn't stop them, and she didn't want to.

Regan stood and paced the small room. "I knew I had to give you up to save you. Curtis told him I had died in the attack, and Michael fled the country. It was stupid. We should have had him locked up, but at the time..." she stopped and looked at Darcy, "all I cared about was you."

"Me?" Darcy got to her feet. "If all you cared about was me, why did you give me away? Why did you turn your back on me?"

"I didn't turn my back on you. I gave you away so he couldn't find you. They told him you were dead, too. There was no reason for him to ever go looking for you and hurt you. You had a good family, and you were safe."

There was no argument for that. She certainly did have a good family and never in her life had she felt threatened.

Regan wiped at her eyes. She was crying now, hard. "I loved you so much. Giving you away was the hardest thing I ever did. Having you back hurts so much, you can't imagine."

There was a sinking feeling in the pit of her stomach, and the ache in her heart was different. "I never meant you any pain. I had no idea, not one, that you might have been the person I was looking for." There was no way she was going to tell her that she had actually thought perhaps her husband had been her father. No good could come out of that.

"I didn't say it was a pain I wouldn't endure." Regan walked toward her. "You're here, in my life. It would hurt even worse to know I knew you and that you walked away."

"I don't belong here."

Regan took her hand and turned it so that the tattoo showed. "You do." She pulled Darcy into her arms and held her.

Darcy wanted to be strong and just stand there, but she

couldn't. A deep, hard sob broke free. She wrapped her arms around Regan and held her tight.

"Darcy, you are my daughter. I don't ever want to lose you again. I won't. I didn't want to lose you the first time. I don't want to do it again."

She wanted to speak. She did. But the words were buried in her throat.

Regan pulled back and wiped the tears from Darcy's face. "Ed will come around. He will."

Darcy only nodded, though she wasn't sure.

"I want you to stay in Nashville. I think we need each other."

Darcy nodded again. She didn't want to leave. She wanted to be Regan's daughter. She did belong to the family she loved so much.

"Spencer and Tyler are a bit confused right now. Zach took them home, and they're having a very long talk."

"I never thought about all this when I went looking for you."

"How could you ever have imagined?"

"They're going to hate me."

"They liked you just fine. You'll be even more important to them."

The moment sunk in. "I have brothers."

Regan laughed through her tears. "They are amazing boys. Amazing."

"Now I know why I was so comfortable around them."

"And why you all have the same eyes." The voice came from the door.

Both Darcy and Regan turned to see Ed standing there. His hair was mussed, and his shirt untucked. He almost looked like he'd been in a fight.

The pain in Darcy's chest deepened as she looked at him. She loved him so much, but how could they possibly ever go back to the way they were?

"I'm going to head home and see if I can help the boys

through this." She kissed Darcy's cheek. "I've missed you so much. I think, if you'll have me, I'd like to take over where your mother left off. And she did a wonderful job, by the way."

Darcy sucked in a breath. "I'd like that."

"Come by for dinner tomorrow. Spend some time with the boys. You'll all need to heal over this. And you should do it together. You're blood."

They were. Oh, she had brothers. Her head spun and she thought she might even pass out, but it was exactly what she'd wanted.

Regan pulled her in for one more embrace and then turned to Ed.

She walked toward the door and stopped in front of him. "None of this is easy. On you, on her, or on any of us. Decisions were made twenty-five years ago, and now we have to face this."

Ed wasn't looking at her. He was looking at the floor.

Regan lifted his chin until he looked at her. "She is my daughter, and I love her very much. Eduardo, I love you, too. Look past what I did, and listen with your heart."

She patted his cheek and walked out, leaving two very hurt people alone to work out their differences.

CHAPTER 47

*E*d stood at the door, and Darcy stood across the room. Neither of them spoke for what seemed like eternity. He was too mad, too hurt, too confused to even form words.

"If you're just going to stand there and breathe, maybe you should go," Darcy said to finally break the silence.

"Maybe you should just let me breathe. I've gone through a lot of hell in the past two hours over you."

"You? You've gone through hell? My whole world just fell in on me."

"You got what you wanted."

"I didn't want to lose you in the process."

Ed raked his sore fingers through his hair. "You don't want me. Not now."

Darcy threw her hands in the air. "I said I didn't want to know. I stopped searching. I came clean with everything I ever knew and all the things I did. I didn't bring this on. You did."

Guilt rolled in his stomach and made him sick. "Christian did it. He asked Curtis to look at the file."

"You're blaming him?"

He took a defiant step toward her and stopped. "I'm telling

you what he did." He retreated back. "I didn't stop him though. I was curious."

"I have very mixed emotions about this. I got what I'd wanted. And I couldn't have asked to have found out that a better person gave me away. Her reasons were very valid."

"I know."

"You have to believe me. I had no idea."

"I know."

She narrowed her stare on him. "What happened to you? You look like hell."

Ed felt like hell, too. "I punched my brother."

"You what?"

He tucked his hands into his pockets as if to hide the marks. "He came at you. I didn't like how he handled the situation."

"Oh, for your information, Eduardo Keller, your reaction wasn't stellar."

"I wasn't ready for that."

"And you think I was?"

He dropped his shoulders. "No."

"Why are you here?" She turned and picked up a box and stacked it on another. "Because I have things to do if you're just going to stand there. I need to move."

"You're not moving."

She stood straight and put her hands on her hips. "Did he punch you back? You have a bruise on your cheek."

Ed touched his face and winced. "Yeah."

"Good. You both deserve it."

She was right. They'd both acted like jerks. But really, who was prepared for that? But he had to remember, she hadn't been prepared for it either.

"This wasn't probably a very good birthday, was it?"

"Oh, I don't know," she said as she plopped down on the couch. "This morning I was wildly in love. I had cake and balloons. Even for a brief, oh, five minutes, I was engaged with a beautiful ring. So most of the day was good. I did meet my mother. I suppose that should make up for it all."

"Darcy, I'm sorry. I should have stopped him."

"You had no idea." The anger had gone out of her fight, and her words were soft.

Ed laughed. "You're my cousin."

"Only by association."

"Darcy, I was joking."

He walked around to stand in front of her.

"I was an ass. I want you to forgive me."

"I don't know if I can. You don't trust me."

Ed knelt down in front of her. "I've been set straight."

She let out a snort of a laugh. "Really? In just two hours you've decided you're fine with this?"

"My grandmother, with a cane, can be very persuasive."

She covered her mouth and chuckled behind her hand. "Did she hit you, too?"

Ed took her hands in his. "In my thirty-five years as a Keller, I have never heard my family scream and yell. Tonight I did. And they were all screaming and yelling at me."

"I'm sorry."

"Darcy, they all love you. What Regan—your mother—went through was terrifying for them all. She did the best thing for you, and she has paid the ultimate price for it. I had no right to treat you the way I did."

Darcy reached up and touched his sore cheek. "You don't hate me?"

"I couldn't hate you. I've never loved anyone as I've love you."

"What are we going to do about all this? I'm here to stay. I'm part of this family now."

He turned her arm over and looked down at her tattoo. He raised it to his lips and brushed a kiss over the words. "You were always a part of it. Darcy, I can't let you go. I never should have said all those nasty things to you."

"It was in your heart at the time."

"No, my ego." He moved in closer to her, still on his knees. He pulled the ring from his pocket and looked at it. "I'm lucky I didn't lose this. My truck is kind of a mess."

"What happened to your truck?"

He winced. "I wrecked it."

"Ed!" She pulled her hands back and covered her mouth. "Tell me you're kidding."

"Wish I was. Oh, how I wish I was." He gripped the ring in his hand. "I couldn't think. I wanted to get here so fast. You're a strong-headed woman. I was afraid you would be gone before I could get to you." He looked around the room. "And from the looks of it, I almost didn't make it."

"If Regan hadn't arrived, you would have been too late."

"Thank goodness she ran out too." He looked at the ring again. "This belongs to you."

"Maybe we should wait so that…"

"I can't wait. Now that I've calmed down and I see what doors have opened, what good it has all brought about, I don't ever want to wait."

He slid the ring back on her finger. "We might have to wait on a date. You and your family need to get to know each other. But, Darcy, you belong with me forever. Our life, beyond all this, will be a happy one. I promise."

The tears were in her eyes again, fresh ones without the pain behind them. "I believe you."

"Good." He moved up and kissed her on the lips gently. "Everything which was lost has now been found."

She sighed. "I like that."

"Maybe that can be your family's tattoo."

Darcy laughed. "I think I'd prefer ones that resemble tiny hands and feet."

Ed's body released all the tension that had built up since the moment he'd first put that ring on her finger, hours ago.

"You'll marry me? You'll have babies with me?"

"I will." She kissed him, this time with her newly decorated hand in his hair. Then she rested her forehead against his. "I think we should keep the Keller tradition alive, too."

"What's that?"

"Like you said, what was lost is now found. Perhaps we can find a lost soul who needs us to be his, or her, parents."

His heart swelled so large he thought it might burst out of his chest. "You do belong in this family. My grandmother was right."

EPILOGUE

*D*arcy stood in the bedroom of her birth mother's home and looked into the antique mirror. The dress she wore had belonged to her grandmother—Alice Keller.

"You look stunning," Regan—her mother, Darcy reminded herself, said.

"I think I'm going to be sick."

Regan laughed. "You wouldn't be human if you didn't feel that way."

Darcy noticed the tear that Regan wiped away, and she turned to her, pulling her in for a hug. "I hope those are happy tears."

Regan chuckled as she squeezed Darcy tighter. "I never could have imagined I'd know who you are, let alone be here with you on your wedding day."

Darcy eased back and looked at her mother. "Something tells me that we would have crossed paths."

"I'm sorry your mother isn't here," Regan said.

"She's with me in spirit. And considering my father is here, and seems to have made himself very comfortable around every-one, I think he's okay with me being part of this family too. It'll never diminish the life they gave me."

Regan kissed Darcy's cheek. "I think we'd better go down and get you married."

Ed paced in Zach's home office while Christian watched him.

"You're making me dizzy," Christian complained as he rubbed his knee.

"Well, don't let me bother you on this important day to you."

Christian croaked out a laugh. "God you're a moody bastard."

"I want it all to be perfect. She deserves perfect."

Christian stood and walked toward Ed. "It is perfect. Even if you trip or faint while giving your vows, it's perfect."

And Ed wondered when Christian had become so wise.

"Thanks."

When their father and Zach walked through the door, they both turned.

Zach held out a glass to each of them. "It is tradition to have a drink before you get married in my garden."

Ed laughed. There had been many happy marriages that started in the Benson rose garden, including his parents' second marriage.

Zach filled each glass with two fingers of brandy. "Here's to the best prodigy I could ever have asked for. May your marriage be as blessed as mine has been, and your parents."

Darcy stood with her father, her arm looped through his.

"You're shaking," he said in his cool military tone.

"I'm nervous."

He gave her hand a pat. "We can turn around and walk out the front door."

Darcy chuckled. "I'd never dream of it." She turned to face

him. "I want to thank you for embracing Regan and her family. I know that can't be easy on you."

Her father pressed his hand to her damp cheek. "When you love someone else's child as much as we loved you, you know that there is a chance you'll have to share them someday. I couldn't have asked for a better family to share you with."

Darcy leaned in and kissed her father's cheek. "I love you."

"I love you too," he said and she could hear his voice catch. "Let's get you married."

Ed stood in the rose garden, his palms wet and his heart pounding as Darcy and her father walked toward them. Christian's wide smile hand't gone unnoticed, but when Ed looked again, he was smiling at Victoria, whom he'd been dating.

His mother wiped away tears, and so did his father. Regan wrapped herself around Zach's arm, and both of Darcy's brothers' wore enormous smiles.

The situation was odd, he could admit that, but what were the Kellers but eclectic.

When Darcy and her father reached him, her father kissed Darcy's cheek, then turned to him. "Take good care of our girl."

"That's a promise," Ed said as he took Darcy's hand. "You're shaking," he said to her as they turned toward the minister.

"There's a lot of pressure to become a Keller," she whispered.

"You are a Keller," he said and chuckled.

"It's an honor on both sides. And to think, I'll carry the name now, and bring more Kellers into the world."

Ed lifted her hand to his lips and kissed it. "Then let's get this over with so we can start working on that."

LOVE SONGS

We hope you enjoyed Bernadette Marie's
Lost and Found.
Continue the family saga with an excerpt from book six,
Love Songs.

LOVE SONGS

CHAPTER ONE

*C*ould the sun possibly be any hotter, or brighter, or…

Warner's brakes screeched as he came to a stop at the stoplight he'd nearly run though. The glare from the hood of his Ford was blinding. The sweat on his neck was annoying. And the fact that he'd just been told he had no talent, well that was pissing him off.

He had talent. He had a butt-load of talent. Warner Wright had performed on every stage in Nashville. Oh, he'd performed with some of the biggest names when they were begging for a job.

He let out a breath. So why had he been passed up?

Oh he knew why!

The reputation of his family came long before he started trying to sell his songs. One thing about being the ex-stepson of Patricia Little, was all of Nashville knew she was trouble. And even if you were a thirty year old man, and you hadn't had the woman in your life since your own father committed suicide when you were twelve, those things stick in the minds of some. It didn't help that after his father's death, she married a little bigger —a little richer—and soon she'd made it into the bed of The OX,

Harley Oxbury. The only problem was he was Nashville royalty —and married to Nashville royalty. The legend was when Christine Eaden found out about Harley and Patricia she put a shotgun to his crotch and threatened to dismember him.

Did it matter to the world that his ex-stepmother took down one of Nashville's icons? Oh, yeah. The OX lost his career. Record companies didn't want him anymore. The public didn't want to see his shows. There wasn't a product willing to put his name out front. Patricia Little had ruined the icon and her reputation, twenty years later, she was tarnishing his.

Perhaps he needed to change his name.

That was stupid. His name was fine. The woman was only his step mother for two years. By now the town should have forgotten the men she left in her path. Well they probably would have if she hadn't gone on TV and done one of those reality shows where Warner's picture was prominently displayed on her mantel as some kind of trophy of the husbands and "others'" children she left in her wake. And hadn't he asked the producers to take that down? Only a million times.

Well, some people were meant to be on stage and some behind the scenes. The guitar on the passenger seat was a reminder that he was one of them.

Although Jordan Farr, the head of Master Records, told him if he could get a voice to back up his music, maybe the world would start to see past his relation to Patricia Little. That had been the most positive feedback he'd received yet.

The light turned green and Warner eased off the clutch and onto the gas. The truck hiccupped and then picked up speed.

But in Nashville afternoon traffic, he didn't make it far. Warner eased to a stop at the next light.

He could hear the music which the city had been built on. It poured out of the stores and the bars. But this music was closer and the voice wasn't Carrie Underwood's or Miranda Lambert's. No this was fresh, sweet, original, and very close.

Warner turned his head to the right and spotted a woman in a Jeep tapping her fingers on the steering wheel. The song wasn't one he'd heard on the radio. It wasn't a karaoke cut either. No, she was singing to someone's music, and she was magnificent.

She turned her head as if she might have felt his stare. Her dark hair was pulled back in a ponytail. The aviator glasses shielding her eyes reflected his beat-up blue pickup truck.

She stopped singing and smiled. And it wasn't just any smile. It was the kind that came with a wink, if he could have seen her eyes.

That moment nearly stopped his heart, just as her voice had. If he had her by his side then the doors of this town would open up to him.

The woman eased through the intersection and turned right at the next light.

He had to follow.

Warner checked his mirrors and quickly changed lanes. It was a close call with a Mustang, of all things, and the driver flipped him the middle finger. But he had to keep her in his sight.

He made a right, but her Jeep wasn't on the street.

"Damn!" He smacked the steering wheel.

But just then he saw the Jeep. The woman was climbing out of it.

Warner made a U-turn, again causing a car to blare its horn at him and that driver to flip him off. The heat must be getting to everyone. They were all in such a nasty mood.

She'd parked in front of a theater and was jogging up the steps.

Warner screeched to a halt in the middle of the street and pulled his brake. The woman turned around on the steps of the theater and stopped.

He climbed across the bench seat to the passenger door and hung his head out the window.

"Hey," he yelled like some back woods yokel.

"Hey, yourself." She had an accent. She was native and that might be iffy. If she grew up in Nashville then she knew all about the shame of his family. But he'd let that find its own moment. This one was his.

"I'm not stalking you. I swear."

"If you say so," she said slowly, but she didn't make a move toward the street and he didn't blame her.

"I heard you singing. You're freaking amazing."

She laughed and her ponytail waved behind her. "I appreciate that."

"No, really. I know what I'm talking about." He tried to open the door, but it wasn't going so well.

She'd taken another step toward the building. He was losing her.

"Wait. I want to talk to you." Finally he managed the handle and nearly fell out of the truck, which he'd left running

The woman had made it to the top of the steps and gripped the knob on the front door of the theater.

"I'm not crazy. Please hear me out," he was begging, but at least common sense had kicked in enough and he stopped moving toward her. "I'm a song writer. I'm looking for a voice."

The woman nodded slowly, but she didn't make any more moves to run away. That was a positive sign, wasn't it?

"What's your name?" she called down to him.

"Warner. Warner Wright."

"Warner Wright the song writer? Cute."

"No, that's really my name." He took one step further toward the curb. "You have an amazing voice."

She looked at the watch on her wrist then back up at him. "You gathered that from hearing me in my truck?"

"Yes."

Again, she nodded slowly. "Listen, I'm going to be late. If you want to come in and sit that's fine. But I'm out of time for talking on the street."

She opened the door to the theater and walked inside.

Warner started for the door and then the grumbling of his truck caught his attention. God, was he this desperate?

He hurried back to the truck, climbed in, and parked it down the street.

PLEASE REVIEW

We hope you enjoyed *Lost and Found* by Bernadette Marie.
If you did, we would ask that you please rate and review this title.
Every review helps our authors.

Rate and Review: Lost and Found

ABOUT THE AUTHOR

Bestselling Author Bernadette Marie is known for building families readers want to be part of. Her series The Keller Family has graced bestseller charts since its release in 2011. Since then she has authored and published over fifty books. The married mother of five sons promises romances with a Happily Ever After always…and says she can write it because she lives it.

Obsessed with the art of writing and the business of publishing, chronic entrepreneur Bernadette Marie established her own publishing house, 5 Prince Publishing, in 2011 to bring her own work to market as well as offer an opportunity for fresh voices in fiction to find a home as well.

When not immersed in the writing/publishing world, Bernadette Marie can be found spending time with her family, traveling (mostly to Disney parks), and running multiple businesses. An avid martial artist, Bernadette Marie is a second degree black belt in Tang Soo Do, and loves Tai Chi. She is a retired hockey mom, a lover of a good stout craft beer, and might have an unhealthy addiction to chocolate.

www.ingramcontent.com/pod-product-compliance
Lightning Source LLC
Chambersburg PA
CBHW031105030726
47496CB00002BA/393